Fated Absolution

Aaron's Kiss Series Book 6

KATHI S. BARTON

WCP

World Castle Publishing, LLC
Pensacola, Florida

Copyright © by Kathi S. Barton 2012
ISBN: 9781938243189
First Edition World Castle Publishing, LLC, April 5, 2012
http://www.worldcastlepublishing.com

Cover: Karen Fuller
Photo Shutterstock
Editor: Brieanna Robertson

Chapter One

"You'll go on this assignment or else." Robert Button's face was bright red; his jowls were shaking as were his fists. Maddy was sick and tired of fighting with this stupid little man every day. If it weren't for the fact that she was the best damn researcher he had on staff, he'd fire her ass, and she knew it.

They were standing in his office on the twelfth floor of the Schaller and Schaller law offices. The office like the man was overdone and pompous as far as Maddy was concerned. The couch also like the man was overstuffed and sausage link like, even the colors were about the same, his suit and the couch; the carpet was pale yellow just like his beady little eyes that now that she noticed were set way too close together. He wore clothes that she could swear she saw that pimp on Twenty Second Street wearing the other night when she was on her way home. And he had more rings on his fingers than what was on display at the local jewelers. He was in a single word a Prick.

"I have things to do. I've said that nine times now. I'd think you'd of gotten it already. I am not going out to this client's house and I am not doing it on my own time."

Maddy thought this man represented every vile thing a person could think of and then some. She had a life damn it, not a great one, but it was hers.

He stared at her for about three minutes, and then smiled that smile that didn't say *'hey, let's be friends'* but rather *'I'm gonna have you for lunch'* Maddy really hated that smile. He had her and she knew how too; it was the same threat that he used everytime. He had to pull out the one thing that pissed her off more than anything else, the only thing that would make her cave into his demands.

"If you don't go, then I will simply renew your contract with us or you quit. Either way we win. Breach of contract or let's see I'll add, oh let me see, eighteen more months onto it. No! I think I'll just make it an even twenty four." He wasn't very bright she thought, not bright at all.

"Eighteen is an even number you moronic ass hole. I hate you. I really hate you and this fucking job. I wish everyday that I would have turned down your offer and never worked for you and this fucking firm. You have never, in the four years I've worked for you played fair. I hope I get hit by a car on the way there and you will be stuck with having to do all of your work by yourself or better yet, you get hit by the bus."

"Here's the address, and don't be late. Oh by the way, I loathe you as well. And the day I can get fulfill my contract where you are concerned will be the happiest day of my life."

Maddy Harm had come to work for this firm straight out of law school having been at the top of her class, as well as the youngest graduate in more years than anyone knew. Schaller and Schaller had made the promise that they would help her pay back her student loans, all three hundred and fifty six thousand dollars' worth and she would work for them at a standard rate for two years. Slave wages really when the expected you to work eighty hours a week and to do whatever they asked without question. She had been a very naive twenty years old even for a lawyer, so with stars in her eyes she agreed. But nothing they had promised had been real. Their idea of helping her with the loans was to give her a job, no extra money to pay the loan, just the job, and they took twenty five percent from each check to pay to her lenders after taxes. Then something she didn't realize until fourteen months into the contract was that they had sole option to renew without notice. She knew about the option, just didn't know how they would use it, so everytime something happened. They were adding on another few weeks to months extra to her what she had come to call her prison sentence. And there wasn't a damned thing she could do about it.

There had been the time she had been sick, as everyone at the firm had been, they had added on one week for every day she was off. She had missed a filing deadline, three months more. No one had cared that the deadline had been missed because she wasn't aware that she was supposed to be the one filing the riff, and that it hadn't even been her case, none of that mattered at all to them. Now four years, three months and nineteen days later, she still fucking worked for them, not that she was counting. She'd tried everything, but her pride in herself and her unwavering work ethic kept her from sabotaging herself completely by doing a poor job.

Maddy graduated from college with a fine arts degree when she was barely sixteen, young and very pretty she worked summers at the local 'Y' as a life guard until she could afford to pay for a second hand car that she still used and it was old when she bought it. Her long curly blond hair, voluptuous figure and periwinkle eyes would have opened a great many doors for her, but most of them led to some man's bedroom, and on a few occasions a women's too that would have her working flat on her back. So she went to college the old fashioned way, hard work and study. Maddy had a slight advantage over a lot of students that were older, in that she had a photographic memory. No matter what she heard, read or saw, she could recall it with perfect pitch, diction or clarity. It had served well then and better now.

She gathered up her things from her work area where she spent most of her day and left the building. Her cubby hole, as she called it, was on the fourth floor in the back of the building, and it didn't even have a little window to let in a breeze once in a while, or the sunlight. She couldn't call it an office, as it was just a long table set up in the research area with floor to ceiling books on all the walls, the carpet was so worn there wasn't any nap in several places and it smelled odd. A smell so dank, some days she thought there might have been something dead under the floors. There was no phone, not even a decent desk lamp, just the cheap clip on thingy she'd gotten on clearance somewhere. She didn't even have a company computer, but used the second hand laptop she had bought for school six years ago. It was slow and out of date, but all she had. She couldn't even afford a decent bag for her stuff, but carried everything in a grocery store recycle bag to and from the office every day.

She had gone to see the owner, Mr. Sherman Schaller, the fifth once about the shabby treatment she was getting, and had nearly been disbarred the next afternoon. The only reason she hadn't been was the fact that she had agreed to shut up and do the job she was hired for and to stay out of his personal office. That had been her last time on the top floor and her one and only time invited in the inner circle to date. She hoped to keep it that way. It was his threat the next afternoon that still gave her goose bumps.

"Learn anything? Or would you like another lesson in keeping your big mouth shut? I don't have the time, nor do I care to be bothered by your petty shit, Ms Harm. And everything about you is petty if it doesn't bring me in any billable hours. So remember this the next time you think to complain to me."

Mr. Schaller had inherited the firm from his father, who had from his father. Maddy didn't think any of them had ever been in a court room, wouldn't know how to get there without a driver to take them. She herself had only had one court appearance and that case hadn't won her any favors with anyone on the top floors. It was the trial of a homeless woman, Shade Doe who had been witness to the death of child and the brutal rape of another. She had done the case in her spare, what little there was, and pro-bono. The case had been dismissed on evidence.

"I learned that this is the worse firm in the city to work for and that no one will help me get out of this mess." She was dirty, tired and just didn't give two shits about them anymore.

"Well then, with the exception of the worse firm, you learned what I wanted you to. You will keep doing the job you were hired to do and you will do it with the same integrity and dedication as before. Or, I will have your name smeared all over this town as a thief and anything else I can think of and you will never be a lawyer anywhere. Do I make myself clear?"

"Perfectly." After that Maddy was never without her recorder. Everytime someone opened their mouth to say a word to her, she was recording it. She had hundreds audio cd's filled with daily comments made to her, mostly about her, but sometimes about a client. Against the law? Yes it was, but so was their treatment of her. Sometimes you needed to work fire against fire.

She looked up the address on the map she always had in her car and consulted her compass and headed toward the client's home, she hoped. For a really smart person, she had a terrible sense of direction; actually it was a negative sense of direction. Maddy knew from experience that she would have to stop at least twice to ask for directions and look on the map a minimum of four more times before she got there. She couldn't tell north from South with a compass and leaving early for an appointment had not only become a habit, but a necessity. And most times, while she wasn't late to her appointments, she was showing up right on time.

'Great! They live in the riches part of town. Oh well, my car will be easy to find among the Hummers and Audi's.'

She also talked to herself. A bad habit but her grandmother had done the same thing. She had claimed that it was because she was the only one who gave her the answers she wanted to hear. That became more true the more she worked for this flipping firm. Grammie had died three months ago, and Maddy still missed her horribly.

'Okay, here we are. Oh great, a friggin gate. I certainly hope my window goes back up, you pretention prick.'

Her car was older than she was and had been slowly falling apart for years. But what did you expect when your car was thirty one years old and no one made or carried parts for it anymore. She pushed on the intercom button and waited.

"Yes, may I help you please?" A disembodied voice came over the speaker just outside the address she needed to go.

"Yes, please. My name is Madison Harm; I'm with the law firm of Schaller & Schaller. I'm here to see a Mr. MacManus. I have an appointment."

At least she hoped she did, it would be just like Butt Hole to send her out here on a wild goose chase just to make her look stupid. They had done that once before, set up a luncheon with someone at a nice restaurant and when she had gotten there the man had no idea who she was or what she was doing there.

"Oh, yes Miss Harm, we have been expecting you. Please stand ready and I shall endeavor to get this opened for you momentarily. Just follow the drive up to the house and I shall meet you there."

'*Endeavor*? *Momentarily*? Who are these people, and what century are they from?' As the gate slowly opened to reveal the manicured lawns she whistled under her breath, 'figures, she thought out loud, 'I just bet there's a house to match all this expensive yard work'.

Maddy drove the one mile up to the biggest house she'd ever seen. When she parked her car as far away from the garage as she could, 'don't want the other cars to get jealous of you baby,' after patting the hood, she grabbed her Wal-Mart bag, and the file she was to have Mr. and Mrs. MacManus go over and sign. She almost left her laptop in the car, but decided to bring it in case there were any changes that needed to be made to the document since she had written it. She could make them at once and not need to come back out anytime soon, provided she could use their printer. The firm did not help out with gas money when they sent her out on these extra little duties.

She was met at the door by, one could only assume the butler, a man named Duncan, and led to a very nicely appointed office/study. There were windows everywhere, covered now against the late evening sun. The room was done in earth tones, blues, golds, teals and reds, and soft materials and textures. Several chair groupings and tables were scattered about the room, with large plush pillows scattered about the room's rug covered floor. Along the other walls were shelves, brimming over with books, pottery and pictures of groups of people Maddy assumed were family. The desk, however, was a mess; papers piled high on it, on the floor around it and even on the one other chair that sat facing the massive sucker.

"How on earth do you work in this mess?" She asked the room in general. As she walked to the business side of it and taking into consideration what anyone might think, she started straightening it up. Duncan told her that his Lordship was running behind and would be here as soon as his mate was free. 'Weird terms buddy.'

Maddy didn't have a clue why she was doing it other than she just knew that if it wasn't done soon, she'd be insane within twenty minutes, or at least insane-er. Organizing came to her as naturally as breathing. She first took a quick inventory of what the paperwork consisted of, bills mostly and a few household repairs, noting in the back of her mind that everything had been paid for within days of the receipt. After that, it was a simple system of putting things where it belonged. She never noticed the beautiful furniture all original pieces to the house and the original owner the previous Master of the realm nor the antique carpet that drew the eye to it and the books, rather it all faded to the background of what she was doing.

Aaron MacManus, his Lordship, was a very well respected as well as feared Master Vampire. He had fought and won a duel to take over this realm some six years ago from Carlos Santchez. The fight was a horrific one and lasted a good deal longer than either vampire had thought it would, both of them giving everything they had to win. But in the end Aaron had decapitated Carlos, killing him and inherited the house, the grounds, subjects and the mess on the desk. Not one bit of this matter when Maddy was in a zone.

~~~

Maddy was crawling on the floor under the desk with twelve neat piles of paperwork in front of her when Aaron walked in, Sara close on his heels. There were also two piles on the chair and three across the sofa seat that she had dragged over when she needed sub files to the ones on the floor separated and six more on the desk. Neither of them said a word, but watched the woman. Her hair had come undone and she had ink smears on her face and hands, in the gabardine pants and silk shirt crawl around and listened to her talk with herself.

"Ah ha! Thought you could hide from me did you? Well, too bad. Who keeps papers from the eighteen hundreds? Shit! You don't go there, you go over here. I think I need to have my head examined, this has got to be the dumbest thing I've ever done. Well, maybe not *the* dumbest, there was that time I took that homeless man in to the hospital to have him looked at, the ungrateful turd. How was I supposed to know he was going to squeeze the crap out of my boob when we'd not gotten but ten feet down the road? Had that bruise for awhile, didn't ya dummy? But dumb, yep, this is pretty dumb."

"Are you referring to the fact that you're talking to yourself, or going through papers that don't concern you?" Aaron watched in stunned silence as she picked up her conversation where she had stopped and continued working on the piles.

"Both I suppose. But the talking to myself usually frightens people enough that they run away from me rather than ask me to explain myself. You know come to think of it, that happens a lot. I haven't the foggiest notion why, I guess it's better than talking to the wall or this nice sofa here, my talking to myself I mean."

The girl hadn't looked up nor stopped doing what she was doing, when she answered Aaron. He could feel her embarrassment and thought it was odd that she didn't seem to let it bother her.

"I see. Well, as it is our house, we won't be leaving, so that leaves you explaining what exactly you are doing on the floor with the papers from my desk. Unless of course the sofa does talk to you…it doesn't does it??"

"No, sadly it doesn't. Can you image the stories it might have if it did? Like, 'oh my, Ms Chair, did you see that woman's butt, it was so huge' then the sofa would have to answer, 'oh no, Sofa honey, she was sitting on my lap and I couldn't see a darned thing'. I don't suppose you'd believe me if I said I was an escaped loony person and this is the one thing that calms me? Or that I have a paper fetish and this is my fix for the week? Hummm, I think I like that reason. No? Well, the truth isn't much better. I'm Madison Harm with the Schaller and Schaller law firm, but please call me Maddy. I'm here to have you go over the Midland contract. Surprise! I'm a lawyer."

Aaron was flustered when she stood up. She was very tall and extremely beautiful. He didn't know why that should shock him other than when he had called the firm holding the properties he wanted to inquire about the woman on the phone indicated that the lawyer coming out had been with the firm for some years. He grinned at her apparent embarrassment. Aaron could hear Sara behind him still laughing. When she had to hang onto his shoulder to keep from falling over from her hysteria, he simply put his arm around her and led her to the couch.

'Great now they'll call in the guys with the straight jacket and butterfly net. Might be better than where I am at now.' She was talking to herself again and Aaron wondered if she did that a lot. He figured she must for she was as comfortable with that as she had been with her embarrassment.

Aaron walked over to his now perfectly set up desk. She had put all the pens in a neat row, all facing the same direction, as was the stapler and tape dispenser. His computer, which he had just purchased two weeks ago, was out of the box and set up to a program he'd never seen before it looked like an accounting spread sheet. The trash can was overflowing with neatly folded, yes folded bits of paper and gum wrappers. He looked at her, with a cocked eyebrow.

"You fold your trash? Maybe I *should* call your firm and tell them that you've been folding my trash and going through my papers and have you fired." A hand on his hips, Aaron was a formable man and he knew it.

Chapter Two

"Wouldn't do you any good to complain, they already think I have a screw loose or two. Actually, they'd just add more time onto my sentence and I'd be there another forty years or so." Maddy grinned back as she spoke, thinking he wasn't so bad for a rich guy.

"Stop teasing her Aaron. You know that you are happy this has been taken out of your hands. Someone had to take over this desk or Duncan was going to take a match to it." The woman walked closer to her with her hand extended. "I'm Sara MacManus, this is my mate Aaron. He has been working on that desk for nearly six years, so if he doesn't thank you, everyone else in this house will. Now he won't complain about it anymore nor will he be calling your boss, unless it's to tell them what a great job you've done already."

"Sure. Whatever. Hummm…well, if you want me to finish up, it'll only take me about five more minutes. These just need to be put into the files, then into the drawers."

She dropped to the floor again and proceeded to put each pile into the folder she had already neatly labeled. The filing cabinet had also been set up, the hanging files color coded, labeled and waiting as well. Opening one of the filing cabinet drawers she started dropping neat stacks of paper into each labeled slot. The top drawer was in alphabetical order and color coded as well, all by month and years.

"I'm sorry were late, well that's not really true. And I do thank you for this. I hate paperwork, and that mess was overwhelming."

Aaron stood over her watching what she was doing. She knew just where each piece of information was and her fingers went to them immediately. Once she had lain the paperwork out she knew where it went in the drawers. Simple once she had everything sorted out.

"Here let me get the contact for you, and you can go over it while I file this crap, I mean your papers away. Overwhelming? Yeah, I can see that. I hate it too, paperwork I mean. But once it's cleared away it'll be easier for you to put the little bits in their home now." She had stood up again and pulled the fat files from under her bag and handed it to him. She'd also brought a copy for Mrs. MacManus as her name was on the contract too. Sitting back down she continued, "The property you've asked about is in receivership, meaning that in this particular case the owner has died and the family, his grandson, in this case actually can't pay the past due taxes much less the mortgage. The original owner died about eighteen months ago and was already two payments behind on the loan and even more on the taxes, so even if the grandson comes up with the back taxes, he'll be over two years into back payments by then. Also he's asking entirely too much for the property, you should offer just over the lien amount, about one percent, I think." She was still sitting on the floor with her feet under her, having finished all but two of the files.

There was a knock at the big door and in came, well they flew really, two kids and the man from the front door. He was carrying a very large tray overflowing with plates and glasses. He

14

sat it down of the credenza and helped the children with each a plate of cookies.

"Careful Miss Lizzy, you do not want to dump it on the young lady. There you go Master Mac, mind your feet, please. May I get you anything to drink Ms. Harm?" Mr. Duncan had been directing these two for some time it seemed to Maddy, much as a general would his troops.

"A glass of water would be awesome, thanks." She grinned at the little boy, Mac he'd called him and winked at the girl Lizzy when they fought over serving her their plate of cookies she intervened. "Sorry guys, but I don't like cookies." She told them quickly before she wore them.

"You don't like cookies? Are you nuts! Everybody likes cookies. I think you're just funning with us. Nobody doesn't like cookies." The little boy said with a wicked grin.

"*Aaron Colin MacManus*" Sara shouted. "Say you're sorry right this minute! People have the right to dislike whatever they like without being ridiculed by you. You don't like a great many things and no one calls you nuts, do they?" His mothers face showed she was shocked and embarrassed.

"I'm sorry, but geez lady, how can you not like cookies?" He didn't look the least bit repentant. Maddy looked over at their dad when she would swear that he growled at his son. With a mental shrug, she turned to answer Mac.

He was gonna be a heartbreaker, if he wasn't already. He looked like a small replica of his dad. His eyes had to be the darkest shade of blue she'd ever seen, almost black. His hair dark and wavy hung slightly over the collar of his light green polo shirt. His shorts were dark green and baggy over long legs and scrapped knees. The little girl was stunning, just like her mom. Her hair and eyes were the on the opposite spectrum of the boys, her eyes were light blue and hair the color of honeyed wheat, and straight as a poker, it hung in two braids that had been through a couple of windstorms by the look of them. She was taller than her brother, but wouldn't be much longer if the height of their dad was any indication. She was wearing a dark green polo shirt and light green shorts.

"I don't like that they're crunchy. Now, a good cake, or better yet a cupcake with about a ton of frosting, hummm, I'm in heaven. And I absolutely love chocolate; I don't even care what it's on or how it's served, just give it to me. And my absolute, mostest favorite thing of all time is pie. Oh I love, love, love pie!!!" Maddy grinned at them; he still had a look of absolute horror on his face.

"My Aunt Sam owns a bakery. She makes the bestest cakes and pies in the whole world. You should have her make you a pie sometime. I bet she would." Lizzy had moved over in front of Maddy and was touching her necklace that hung just inside and below her shirt opening. When she accidently got a little chocolate on Maddy's collar Lizzy looked up. Maddy winked again Lizzy pulled the chain up and looked at the pretty stones.

"Maybe I will. Wait, 'Sam's Baked Goods'? Oh yeah, you're right, they are the best. My Grammies favorite was the Boston cream pie. Sam makes the very best."

Maddy took the locket that accompanied the stones and opened for Lizzy, then handed it back. Her Grammie had given her this locket and chain; the stones she had told her had come from her mother and the locket from her father, it was a gift to and from each other she'd told her.

"This is me when I was about your age," she told Lizzy and when Mac pushed in she showed him too, "and this is my Mother. I don't know her. She died a very long time ago. Just after I was born"

"She's dead? Brent's mommy got dead, but he gots a new one and a daddy too." Lizzy asked her while still fingering the design on the locket.

"I don't know anything about them." Before someone started asking question she wasn't comfortable answering, Maddy changed the subject. "What sort of confection do you guys like?"

"Sometimes Aunt Sam bakes us un-birthday cakes. That's fun. We get to each pick a day and she bakes us what we want."

Each child took a turn holding and looking at the tiny pictures that had been enclosed within the gold locket. When they were both finished, she slipped the chain back into her blouse.

"That *is* very nice, I don't even like to celebrate things when everyone else does, but I bet that would be fun-city to have a special un-day. Mr. MacManus, there are several other properties and businesses in that general area, most of which have all gone belly up. If you wanted to save some real money, I'd approach the lender directly and see if you can get them for about fifty cents on the dollar. Most of them will be willing to take a cut just to not have to carry it on their books anymore. No, no more tea for me please, I have a long drive home. Most of them are just defaulted loans, but quite a few are in for non-payment of taxes, as well."

Maddy set down her tea cup that was a part of the set Lizzy had gotten from the big closet across the room. Maddy went over to the computer on the desk she had set up and pulled up the city map for the area she was talking about.

"This property is in default of their loan, as are these six here. This one and this one are in tax trouble by thousands of dollars, but not default yet, but it shouldn't be much longer. If you'd like I can get you the names of the leaning institutions that are involved and you can see what you can work out."

"As my lawyer, wouldn't you be the better person to do this for me?" Aaron asked.

"Nah, I'm not really your lawyer. Mr. Butt Hole, err…Button sent me out here tonight as punishment. If you want to contact him and have him do it that'll be fine, too. But it will be costly. He'll charge you four hundred an hour and bill you for a minimum of eight hours. Doing it yourself will only take about an hour or so and it's free. I could show you how, it's really easy." Maddy offered as she shut down their computer.

"You don't like your boss." Sara hadn't asked, just made a statement. Maddy didn't care if they knew about her feelings toward her boss, as far as she was concerned her employment couldn't get much worse, just longer. They would add on more months, years, it didn't matter; she was as stuck with them as they were with her. And if she could make them lose a little money in the deal, great! She wouldn't complain.

"No, Mrs. MacManus I don't, but then the feelings are very mutual. I should be going. I have to get home before it gets too dark to read the street signs. I can get lost in my own apartment."

She gathered up her things, and after shaking hands with the adults and getting a surprising hug from the two kids, she left. She'd told them to either call the firm or let her know by her email account it if they decided to do it on their own. She could get them the list as late as tomorrow morning when she got to work.

~~~

"What did you think of Maddy Harm?" Sara had waited until after they had put Lizzy and Mac to bed to sit with the contract that the girl had left them and to discuss it with Aaron. Maddy was all the children had talked about when they had put them to bed an hour ago. And wanted to invite her to their birthday party, the real one in three weeks.

"She's great. Did you get anything from her?" Aaron had truly liked the girl. She was upbeat, honest and the kids had taken to her immediately. And to him that was the great testimony of all kind. Children could spot an insincere person right away.

"Nothing other than she is as honest and sincere as she acts. She does hate her boss though, but I couldn't get the why. Did you get anything?"

Both were telepaths, Sara being the stronger of the two. It had paid them well to be able to 'read' people in dealings whether personal or business. They both had a great many other talents and powers. Sara being the cousin to the Queen of all Magick and Aaron was a fourteen hundred year old vampire, a Master one at that.

"No, just the same. I couldn't believe how well she interacted with the children. But Lizzy crawling up in her lap to play tea with, her that was a shock. She is normally very standoffish with strangers."

Aaron had been amazed. They had played tea party and Maddy had never once seemed impatient nor did she seem to be trying to impress them by interacting with their children.

"Well, how do you want to handle the other properties, buy them ourselves or call Mr. Butt Hole?" Aaron loved that it had slipped out; it showed the girl had a good sense of humor on top of everything else.

"Caught that did you, I nearly hurt myself trying not to laugh out loud. I'm thinking we should do a little investigation into this firm, I think there's something off there. Couldn't hurt, and it may gain us a much needed ally in the legal world with her. I have an old friend that I can call; it's about time for him to visit anyway."

"Aaron honey, I hate to break it to you, but all of your friends are old."

Chapter Three

"Sure, I'd love to visit. It's been what, sixty or seventy years?? Heard you got yourself caught and truly shackled."

Kyle Dixon was really surprised to hear from his oldest friend Aaron. He and Aaron had been turned about the same time, a little over fourteen hundred years ago. Over the ensuing years they had become very close, as close or closer than brothers, coming to the aid of one another whenever the other called. He was also a good friend of Colin Larimore's, having helped with his very touchy change when he been nearly beaten to death for taking the blame for a stolen loaf of bread a woman had taken for her children.

"I have a few things I'd like to go over with you before you look into something for me. Also, if Sara hears you call her a shackle, she cut you to ribbons, and I my dear friend will laugh my ass off when she does."

Kyle was incorrigible. He knew it and so did his friends. But with Aaron, Kyle would freely admit that he dearly loved the man.

They set up a time to meet at the end of the week. Kyle hoped that Aaron would ask him to be a part of his Kiss. He had been wandering for some time now and was ready to settle down. He couldn't' think of any place he'd rather be than with good friends and hopefully new ones.

~~~

"Maddy, I took a phone message for you. Some sexy male voice would like for you to call him back as soon as you can. I told him you were in a meeting. Why that skinflint Schaller won't give you a phone in that dungeon he puts you in is beyond me."

Caroline Peters worked as Mr. Button's personal secretary. She was also sleeping with him. It was a part of the job description. She would work in this position and whatever other position the nasty old man wanted until someone new came along, and then she'd be shuffled off to another part of the building or bought off. She was taking the buy off, Maddy remembered her telling her once, she had big plans for that money and was planning to retire on it, and hell she'd said she was only twenty-nine. Maddy really liked Caroline. Maddy was the only person who treated her as a person, a person of worth, not some two bit whore, she knew. She couldn't help but here the gossip about her. They had never talked about what she did on the side and Maddy certainly didn't want to know either.

"Don't worry about it. This way, when he wants me he has to come to me to yell at me instead of just calling. And I'm sure there are times when he doesn't think it's worth the move off his big butt to do it."

She looked down at the pink message slip and wondered at the name and number. She didn't know a Colin Larimore. Oh well; she'd just have to find a pay phone somewhere.

Twenty minutes later she was still trying in vain to get in touch with him. Her frustration was making her talk to herself more. "If you leave a message to have someone call you back, the very least you could do is be there when they call." She left him a second message.

"Mr. Larimore, this is Madison Harm with Schaller and Schaller again. You called the office today looking for me. I don't have one, an office I mean, nor do I have a phone, cell or otherwise. I will be at this number for another hour. After that, well it's up for grabs. Okay." That said, she hung up.

Maddy hated leaving messages with strangers. You didn't know whether they were a legitimate call or someone cranking your chain from the office, but she trusted Caroline. Plus, she tended to babble when she was nervous, on top of talking to herself; she was a cracker short of a picnic basket.

"You want to tell me why we are taking personal phone messages for you on company time?" She didn't know how long Mr. Butt Hole had been standing there, but from his mood she would guess it had been a while. Did he truly expect people to fall to the floor and kiss his feet when he entered a room? Sometimes she took her time acknowledging him just to piss him off. A girl just had to have fun once in a while.

"Well, as I don't have any friends, I'm pretty sure that it wasn't a personal message. I do, however; have a call into a potential client, a Mr. Larimore. Was it him that called and got your panties all in a bunch?"

Maddy had no respect for Button and didn't bother hiding the fact. She couldn't stand that he was the laziest man she knew and that he would take advantage of every situation. Not unlike most people, but he was particularly good at it.

Rather than answer her, he slammed the slip down on the table and huffed out of the room. He had to have heard her laughing all the way down the hall. She was still grinning when she got to the now empty reception desk to use the phone there.

"Mr. Larimore, please? This is Madison Harm returning his call. He called just a few minutes ago."

She was watching the birds on the tops of the trees while she had waited for the phone to be picked up by him. *Oh to be out of doors on a day like today* she thought, *or to at least have a little window to look out of once in a while, or a nice breeze on a pretty day.*

"Hello Ms. Harm. I'm sorry we have been playing phone tag, but I'd like to talk to you about some property you talked to Aaron MacManus about, he's a good friend of mine. I'm interested in purchasing four of the empty buildings that are on Merchants Way and was wondering if you'd act as mediator for me? I have some daytime conflicts and am unable to call the banks during their hours."

Maddy would have gotten a shock out his "daylight conflicts" had she of known what they were. Colin, like Aaron and Kyle was a vampire. She was blissfully unaware of any non-human creatures.

Vampires didn't really fry to ash when the sun hit them; it heated them up from the inside out. Starting with their bones, it cooked them, boiling their insides to the point of exploding. If they got to ground, or into a deep lair and plenty of fresh blood they could survive, if they hadn't been out too long, but it took weeks, sometimes months for them to recover.

"Sure, but he did explain to you that I don't have my own practice. And that I work for a larger firm. You would have to go through them first before I could legally help you out."

You never knew when the phones were bugged in the office, so she always made sure to cover her butt. She wasn't unethical, just smart.

"Yes, yes he explained all that. You'd only be acting as a go between, but I understand what you are saying. Who would I need to talk to in regards to this? Sara mentioned a Mr. Button, is that who I'd contact? Or Mr. Schaller? I'd like to get started on this right away, Ms. Harm. Is either of them in their office right now?" Apparently Colin had a clear plan and he was the type to forge ahead and get it accomplished, Maddy thought.

"Mr. Button is still in his office as a matter of fact, and he'd be the one you'd contact, yes. I have his direct phone number, so you could call him whenever you want."

"Could you transfer me to him now? I like to do things when I have all the players in front of me Ms. Harm, now would work out very well for me."

Mr. Larimore did indeed want to get the ball rolling. So Maddy called her boss and started to explain to him what Mr. Larimore wanted and that he was on the three-way with her when he got nasty with her. Again.

"You know we aren't a real estate office, right? Out front of the building it says, in very large letters as a matter of fact, 'Schaller & Schaller, Attorneys at Law' no where does it mention 'call us up if you need to have some dumb cunt help you buy some worthless property'. Tell your lover boy that if he wants you to help him, as long as it's on your own time, I don't give a flying fuck what you do." He was actually much nicer this time than he had been in the past; the problem now would be he had a witness.

"Okay, is that your final decision on my helping Mr. Larimore?" Even she could hear the barely concealed humor in her voice, but this was just too great for caution.

"You are a fucking pain in my ass," he practically screamed into the receiver. "I don't give a shit. Did you understand me that time, bitch."

"Did you hear that Mr. Larimore, I have Mr. Button's approval in helping you so long as it's on my own time? Shall we set up a time to get together tomorrow?" Her voice was sugar sweet and ever so polite, and if she sounded just a tad breathless it was because she was holding onto her all out laughter with every fiber of her being. She didn't figure it would be in her best interest to start screaming with laughter at this point.

"Yes, Ms. Harm, that is quiet all right. Mr. Button, you are…there are simply no words to describe you. I run several very, very large corporations and looking for a law firm to help us diversify. If you were the last firm on this Earth I would not use you. And I will be sure to tell everyone I know just what sort of person you are and how you treat your employees. Ms. Harm, I look forward to hearing from you now that we have it established you are a free agent.

Maddy hung up the phone as soon as Colin did and made a dash to her little dungeon, hoping to get out of the building before Mr. Button had a chance to corner her. She didn't make it. She was just picking up her bag and turning when he was right there. His hard slap across her face knocked her backward. She hit her head on the corner of her table as she was going down blackness engulfed her.

Chapter Four

"I'm telling you, you should have heard him, Aaron. He talked to her like she was trash, way beneath him. And the language he used…well hell Aaron, it made me blush to know she was listening."

Colin had been talking about nothing else since he'd gotten off the phone with Maddy. He couldn't abide by them being mistreated, verbally or physically. He loved women all women. But he especially loved Shade, his mate.

"How did she take it, lose her temper? I would have, I'd of gone right into his office and cut his dick off." Sam, Tucker's mate could be a little, well let's just say she didn't have a lot of love for abusive men, women either. She was a part of a large underground system that helped get abused spouses out of their homes and into safer areas. She'd been doing it for years, simply using the bakery as a front.

"Nah, if anything she seemed to think it was funny. I could hear her trying her best not to laugh. She's a gutsy little thing. She's supposed to come by tomorrow night sometime after six. I hope you don't mind, but I'm having her meet me here. She said she had a very bad sense of direction and she'd been here before."

"No, that's great as a matter of fact. There are a few things I'd like to ask her about anyway. Kyle will be here tomorrow too, but I don't expect him until after midnight." Aaron mentally rubbed his hands together. He and Colin needed her help and if Bradley and Kyle were in, they had one hell of a deal for the girl and for themselves.

~~~

'Turn right at the next stop sign and poof, I should be there, ha!! I said that ten minutes ago. You'd think a house that friggin big would be easy to find, especially since I've been there before! But oh no, not for me. Sheesh, Maddy you really could get lost in your own bathroom without a map.'

She still hurt from what Button had done to her last night. She had woke up this morning on the same floor where he'd left her, covered in blood, her blood, and sore as hell. Today her left eye was black all the way down her cheek and her jaw was bruised as well, knowing tomorrow and the next day she be sorer didn't help. She also had a knot the size of a golf ball on the other side of her head that hurt so bad she had left her hair down because pulling it into a pony tail had hurt too badly.

She saw the blur of movement about ten seconds before she hit it. Or it hit her. The car slammed to a stop and jolted her so badly she hit the window with her sore face. This time her nose bloodied as well.

She staggered out of the car and limped over to the heap of dark clothes. It was big friggin heap of clothes too. She knew it was going to have a body in there somewhere and the way her luck was running, she killed the body too. She started reach out and touch when he moaned. She knew it was a male because unless there was something seriously wrong with this woman's vocal cords and she'd been on steroids for, well years, then she was a guy. Well, she thought, at least I didn't kill him, yet.

She fell to her knees beside him, not caring what she was doing to her pants. They were covered in blood anyway. Her shirt was ruined as well; blood from her nose marred the front of it. Her hand had just touched his shoulder when he turned and grabbed her wrist in a tight hold.

"Hey, bones, bones, bones! Well, I guess it's safe to assume you didn't hurt your hand. Let me go, that fucking hurts!"

Maddy started smacking him with her other hand. If he didn't let her go soon, she'd have a broken wrist on top of everything else.

"You hit me…you tried to kill me, well it won't work. It won't be that easy. And you are not going anywhere. I need help."

The man's voice was deep and had an accent that made her spine tingle. But that didn't make her any less pissed off at the stupid man.

"Really? Could have fooled me! I don't know why I didn't think the puddle of blood you're lying in was an indicator of that fact. Dumb ass." She began searching his pants pockets, then his shirt.

"What the fuck are you doing now, looking for a place to stick a knife? My wallet is in my back pocket. Want me to roll over for you so you can rob me easier?"

She noticed that accent again and the fact that it got stronger the madder he got. She was sorely tempted to really make him mad to see if he'd slip into the language that he was falling slowly back into.

"Look you overgrown prick, do you see a knife? I'm looking for a phone. I need to call you an ambulance. I have insurance, not great insurance, but I have enough to cover your injuries; at least I hope I do provided you don't linger in a vegetative state for too long. For just another limb and maybe my left eye I suppose I could have had really good insurance, but silly me, I thought that eating would be more beneficial." She snorted as she was still patting him down when he grabbed her other hand.

"You're weird. No, no ambulance and no police. I'll be fine in a few minutes." He said to her still holding onto her hand. He had laid his head back onto the pavement and closed his eyes.

Maddy looked at him, what else did she have to do when he was holding her hands hostage. His hair was a very dark black, almost blue, it was so shiny. His face was tense now, probably from pain, but no less handsome, a jaw that screamed to be caressed, a nose that was narrow and straight. His mouth was full and sensual, sexy and...holy shit, back up girl. Where the heck had that come from? Picking up their conversation where he'd stop talking she went on.

"Oh. Well of course you will. How stupid of me to be concerned. Well, if you're sure, I'll take my leave while you bleed to death in the middle of the road. Stop being a macho jackass and let me call someone for you."

She struggled in vain to get her hands free, but he just tightened his grip. Her moan of pain stopped him short. It was then that he looked at her.

"You are not going to claim that I did that to you. I do not beat stupid women. I know how your types of women are. Well, you won't get a dime out of me." His voice sounded so bored as if dealing with her 'type' happened to him every day.

Maddy stared at him for all of twenty seconds and jerked her hands from him, his nails tearing into her tender flesh. She stood, staggered for a moment and hobbled back to her car. She was trying her best not to cry. She hurt everywhere. Her nose was still bleeding. Her new pants and shirt were ruined and she had an appointment she was going to be late for. Before she got inside her car, he was already getting in the passenger side. She looked back to where he'd just been to her car again. S*heesh! He could really move fast. Shi*t! Now he was getting into her car. Oh no. No, no he was not.

"What do you think you're doing? Get out of my car, you maniacal bastard! *Get out right now.*

He just ignored her and climbed in. He had to adjust the seat as far back as it would go and then he was still squashed in there like he was a sardine. She knew she couldn't make him budge. She was surprised that he'd even been able to get up. Maddy would have sworn he was hurt really bad. She just got into the driver's side and started the engine. She resolved to not speak to him all the way to her appointment. And she would not take him anywhere else. She just hoped he didn't go into shock or anything while in her car. This was all she needed, a dead man riding around with her. Just her luck Schaller and Schaller would probably be the ones suing her for his family.

"Where are you going now? I have a right to know where you are taking me. Are you going to answer me when I speak to you? Hey! Are you in there?"

He had asked that four times now and she still had not said a word to him. It's not that she didn't speak, she did, but all to herself. Mostly it was to put her down or to comment on the wrong turn she'd taken but never anything directly to him.

When she pulled up in front of the MacManus mansion gate, he started laughing. He was still laughing when she was trying to make herself heard over his laughter into the speaker at the gate.

"Mr. Duncan, its Madi...its hummm...I have an appointment with Colin Larimore and Aaron MacManus. I don't suppose you remember me from last week?"

No way was she giving this guy her name. It was bad enough he'd gone through all her trash, making snide comments about the fact that she folded it nice and neatly, and did you do that for her house trash as well. As a matter of fact she did, but she didn't tell him that. For all she knew he was some sort of mass murderer or a slasher or something equally hideous.

"Oh yes, Miss Harm, we've been expecting you." So much for keeping her name private she thought. She turned to glare at the man next to her when he began laughing in earnest again.

"Did you think I wouldn't get it? What business could you possibly have here? Aaron is a good friend and I won't let you do anything to his reputation or his family." He said this with a sneer and a grin. Who would have thought that was even possible?

"Fucking dick head. All men should all be castrated and left to the wild animals to feast upon." She had been talking to herself and had lowered her voice a great deal, but he had heard her she knew it.

It was nearly full dark when she pulled up in front of the house. She hated driving at night, but this couldn't be helped he'd told her he has a problem that prevented him from working with her during the day and she wanted to be as accommodating as possible for him. She wished now that she had called and rescheduled. She hurt worse now than before she'd hit this man, and she was dizzy too.

As soon as the car stopped he was out and to the door. She was still struggling with her seatbelt when Mr. Duncan was leading the man in. *Well, he must not have been lying when he said he knew the MacManus*. Mr. Duncan came out to help her gather her stuff, but she shooed him off saying she was used to lugging it around. Half way to the door she realized she should have taken his help, she wasn't gonna make it. Stopping not six feet from the doorway, she just couldn't go any further, her entire body was screaming in pain.

"Master Kyle said that you had a slight accident and you may need my assistance. He said that you tried to run him down on an otherwise open highway. I do not believe that for a moment, and told him so."

He simply took her Wal-Mart bag from her in one hand and lead/dragged her inside with the other. It made her happy that someone believed her. But she couldn't concentrate on that right now. Pain riddled her body like bullets being shot into her everywhere.

They were just inside the open hallway when Duncan turned to take a good look at Maddy. She thought she must look really bad if the expression on his face was any indication. He nearly fell over in his haste to take the rest of her things from her and have her sit down in the large church pew right inside of the entrance hall. It was too much, within seconds of his kind words, she was sobbing.

"Oh, Miss Harm, there, there, let me get you something to dry your eyes. Do not move. I will return momentarily." And off he went toward what she could only assume was the kitchen.

She grabbed her big blue Wally World bag and started for the door. She had humiliated herself enough for one night and decided nothing could make her stay. She had the car started and was turning it around when someone slammed on the window next to her. She screamed and jerked around in time to have none other than Master Kyle himself opening her door and turning off her car.

"Get off; what…give me back those keys. I mean it, I've had enough of you for one night and I hurt in places you can't imagine."

When he simply held them over his head, she shut the door on him, nearly getting his hand. The car was on enough of a downhill swing; she just let it roll and popped the clutch. When the engine turned over, she put it into gear and started off. But not before she turned to him and stuck her tongue out at him. Childish? Yes, but she wanted to go home. Too bad she didn't make it much further than a few inches; it was a very nice parting shot though.

Kyle stood in front of her car and she really hoped that she wouldn't run him down, again.

Chapter Five

Instead of running him down like she really, really wanted to, she stopped the car a mere inch from his legs. She missed him falling forward onto her hood, and the heavy sigh of relief that he expelled. He really thought she was going to do it. No, she missed it all because she had laid her head on the steering wheel and started crying harder, harder than he'd ever heard a woman cry before. He hated a woman's tears.

It wasn't until Duncan came out to the car to check on her that Kyle raise his head. He was surprised to see her upset, her crying hurting him for some reason, hurt him deep in his chest. He was the one she'd run down for Christ's sake, what the fuck did she have to be upset about.

"Come now Miss, you must come into the house and let us have a look at these wounds. Let go of the driving devise please, there's a good girl."

Kyle came to lend a hand. He had just reached for her when she turned on him, all claws and teeth. He might have been impressed if he wasn't afraid of hurting her.

"You fucking stupid jackass! Do you have a death warrant? You dumb fucking jackass–"

"You've called me that several times now. You might want to broaden your vocabulary. Or maybe stop calling me names altogether."

He didn't know what possessed him to antagonize her. She was just too beautiful not to, the way her eyes darkened and sparkled. It was everything he could do not to just make her mad to watch them.

"You...why I should...I am going to...shit, I'm gonna pass out."

And she started to crumble toward the hard driveway. Had Kyle not been as close as he was, she would have a few more bruises to add to the array she already had. Instead he grabbed her up into his arms and held her slight body to his larger one as he carried her into the house just behind Duncan.

~~~

"Oh my god, look at her! So help me god if you did this to her I will gladly take your head from your shoulders."

The tiny woman at the end of the bed blazed with anger. The other woman, she smelled of Aaron, simply looked at him. He knew that he was being assessed.

Kyle had the good sense to not say a word, he knew women enough to know that the less one said when they were mad, the less likely they were to take more of your hide off. He did look over to Aaron and sent a mental message.

"I didn't do this, you know that don't you?"

"I'm not even going to justify that with an answer. You know me better than to think I would. Sam has had issues with men who would do such a thing to women and not think anything about it. I will have a talk with her."

"I didn't realize she was this hurt. But damn she can fight. She had no problems taking me on without a thought to how much bigger I am than her."

He could feel the laughter bubbling up from within, but when the little spitfire Sam had turned to glare at him again he quickly turned it into a cough. He thought there was no reason to get himself hurt in the process.

"Someone beat the snot out of her. I would say as late as yesterday. These on her wrist, they are from much earlier though. Probably today I'd say. She has a large contusion on her head, blunt force, her jaw is badly bruised and you can see the amount of bruising on her face." Thomas Reilly the vampire doctor and had stepped into the room just as Kyle had brought Maddy in.

"I am responsible for her wrists." He would admit to that much. He hated that he'd hurt her, but he didn't mean to do it. He'd let his overactive suspicious mind get the better of him. "She and I had a little accident on the way in here and I did the ones marking her wrist. I'm sorry about that."

"No he's not. I should have just left him bleeding in the street and drove over his ass, maybe even backed up a couple of times too."

Everyone looked at the girl as she spoke. She was beautiful despite the bruises. And the glare in her eye made him burst out laughing. She was ballsy, he'd give her that.

"It's just as well, I suppose. You would probably have gotten lost on the reverse trip anyway. How are you feeling?"

Kyle wasn't happy with the feeling she was bringing out in him, one minute he wanted to strangle her, the next, and this was really weird he wanted to take care of her. He *hated* needy women.

She sat up, or at least she attempted to. Dr. Reilly was pushing her back down before she was all the way up. She smacked his hand away and pushed him off the bedside and onto the floor and tried again. Thomas Reilly was the doctor around the realm. Aaron had explained to Kyle and he looked ready to go toe to toe with Maddy himself.

"You try to get up one more time before Thomas says its okay, I'll lie on top of you to keep you there. Understand? You look like someone who has been beat up. What the hell happened to you?"

Kyle was pushing her back down as he spoke. If looks could kill, he was pretty sure he'd have been cut in two by her. He simply grinned at her. Apparently she thought to intimidate him with it, when all it did was make him laugh. And she smelled good. Something he hadn't smelled in centuries, what was that...

"You try that again you sorry excuse for a human being and I will make your children's children regret it. You understand that? How your wife puts up with you is beyond anything. She should be canonized."

Maddy lay back down again. Kyle found himself to be slightly disappointed. He'd thought of lying on top of her sounded damned good. But he couldn't help it, he burst out laughing. He wasn't human and he would probably be around for his children's children, so he'd know firsthand if they regretted her actions or not.

"Kyle, why don't you and Aaron go down stairs and let the Maddy rest?" Sara wasn't fooling anyone. Her lips were twisting into a grin no matter how hard she tried to stop it. Yes sir, this one had fire and Kyle was having a great time.

"Maddy is going home. And I swear to you I'm at the end of my tether in regards to you and your bossy attitude. If you so much as take one step toward me, I will not be responsible for what happens."

She had gotten to a sitting position before Kyle had started toward her again and her statement stopped him cold. Without any assistance from anyone, though she should have taken it, she made it to the bathroom. They all could hear her speaking to herself, their hearing beyond human hearing. Then there was the fact that she didn't seem to care if they heard or not. It was her mimicking Kyle that got Sara finally, loud cackling laughter burst from her so quickly it startled them all.

"'If you get up I'll lie on top of you'. Not bloody likely you arrogant macho pig headed jerk. As if I need their permission to go home. I've been driving myself for a long time. I'll thank you very much. Of course, I get lost everywhere I go, so I guess that makes me have more practice. Yeah that's it! I really need to find a nice man and settle down. Yeah right! Like I'd let that happen. Men suck!"

Maddy opened the door to find Kyle standing against the door jamb waiting for her. She moved over to the chair without giving him any indication she'd even seen him and went about putting her shoes back on, which had blood on them too. Brushing away a tear she stood up and walked toward the door he was currently blocking.

"Move."

"I'm taking you home." Kyle was trying not to laugh at her but at the same time show her he was the man and she should bow down to his superior knowledge. *Yeah*, he thought, *I'm arrogant.*

"Move out of my way." Maddy said each work like a vow. A vow that said, you either do it or face the consequences. He really wanted to see what she'd do if he pushed her.

"Are you listening to me? I said I'm taking you home. You're in no shape to drive and as long as it would probably take you to get there, I could drop you off and be back before you'd get there. Now shut up and get your things and we'll leave now." There, now she would understand he meant business.

When he moved she walked past him without a single word. Moving down the staircase, she paused long enough to look around the beautiful room spread out below her. When she noticed him looking at her she put her nose in the air and moved down again. Instead of going toward the front door where he assumed she was headed, she moved to the right. He thought it was the kitchen. It was the kitchen and Mr. Duncan was there as well, looking up when they entered the room.

"I would like you to call the police for me. I'm being harassed by this man. He has accused me of running him over–"

"You did run me over!" Now she had gone too far he thought.

"Well of course I did. Can you just see it Mr. Duncan? I drove up on the sidewalk. I ran him down, and then I dragged his oversized body out into the street just in time for it to bleed all over the place. Can you just see that, me dragging your big friggin body around? I think not. Mr. Duncan, would you please make that call for me?" Her voice was low and cool, belying the steely intent.

Kyle growled at her. She just turned to look at him with a perfectly shaped raised eyebrow. He'd finally had enough. He took her hand and dragged her out of the kitchen and into the large dining area. When he saw Aaron start to ask him something, he raised his hand to stop him and continued pulling Maddy along behind him. Suddenly she stopped. When he turned to…well that thought didn't finish as she took that opportunity to punch him in the nose. He jerked back, but didn't lessen his hold on her hand.

"*Stop*! Stop right this minute, or so help me I will hit you again. I am not some…some puppy that you can drag to and fro. From the moment you stepped—and I swear you'd better not say a

40

single word, stepped in front of me you have done nothing but torment me, boss me around and lord over me. I am not going to take it from you, do you hear me?"

"I believe the whole house heard you. Now you will—"

She screamed. Not one of those, squeaky little shrieks that some women made, no this was a full blown, hair standing on end, ear hurting, piercing scream. When she inhaled to do it again, he did the only thing he could think of. He pulled her to him and kissed her.

Chapter Six

She stiffened in his arms, her whole body rigid against his. And when he made to pull her in closer, she put her hands on his chest to push him away, her mouth just opening to give him a piece of her mind he was sure. He took advantage and invaded, his tongue sweeping inside of her mouth tasting and taking. Any thought he'd had completely disappeared. She was his. He cupped her face, tilting her slightly so he could dive deeper, taste more of her when she moaned. That's when he remembered her injuries, her wounds.

He jerked away, pushing her away from him, out of reach because the temptation was nearly overwhelming to pull her back and begin again. He could only look at her, panting with need, need that was slow to dissipate. He closed his eyes against the red haze. He wanted her, but didn't want to frighten her.

"I'm sorry." He wasn't sure why he was, but he definitely was very sorry. He was sorry for kissing her, and for stopping, sorry for pushing her away and not pulling her back; mostly he was sorry he couldn't finish what he so desperately wanted. He wanted her, wanted to be deep inside of her, right now. And she smelled of cherry blossoms. Fuck!

~~~

Maddy, still trying to catch her own breath, finally got her mind to being to function again, it having left the building right along with Elvis finally grasped what he had said. 'He was sorry, he was sorry, he was sorry', like a litany it kept running like an endless loop through her brain. He'd kissed her and now he was sorry.

She turned on her heel and left the room, only to run into Mr. MacManus and the entire household was there as well. They must have came when she screamed she reasoned, came to see what she was about, she wasn't sure anymore. She just needed to get out, out right now before the dam of tears she was barely able to hold in check fell. With a murmured 'sorry, excuse me' she ran to the front door and out into the night. She was into her car in record time and had the door slammed shut and locked seconds after getting in. Damn it!

He still had her keys.

Putting her car in neutral, she stood outside the doorway, with anger and humiliation giving her added strength; she pushed it further down the slight hill. When she was going almost too fast to keep up she hopped inside, popped the clutch again and it thankfully started. Slamming the door, she drove to the gate, which had an eye for giving guests a straight shot out of the drive. She didn't even slow down, but drove faster, as if the man who said he was sorry for kissing her was about to come out and try to stop her again.

There was a note on her table when she came back in to work on Monday. Simply put she was to come to Mr. Schaller's office as soon as she got there. She didn't even bother taking off her light jacket or putting down her things but went up to his offices on the top floor. Her mood had not improved over the weekend nor had her pain lessened.

Wouldn't want to be seen mingling with us underlings, now would we? She'd noticed on Sunday afternoon that she had started having bitter conversations with herself, either centered on the incident at the mansion, or about the fucking duckweed at the house. She had also worked on her vocabulary as he had suggested, coming up with all sorts of creative names for him. She hoped that sometime in the near future she would be able to use them on him.

The bosses latest bimbo, this one had to be number sixteen, was at her desk, eating a donut she didn't need while sipping coffee from a company mug. The coffee smelled like vanilla and something else that said 'I spent more money on this one pound of coffee than you spent on your groceries this week' smell. The office area was tastefully done, warm and cool colors, wood desk and plants everywhere. This area said, 'yes, I'm a very successful lawyer, and you should trust me.' Bullshit!

"Sherman, err Mr. Schaller expected you thirty minutes ago, Ms Harm. I'll see if they're ready for you." Before she could press her little intercom button Maddy commented, not caring anymore if they added two hundred years or two thousand. She'd had enough. Disbarment was much better than what she had had to stoop to do keep her job.

"As I'm not supposed to be here until nine and it's barely eight fifteen, I don't know why he would expect me long before I'm supposed to be here. Unless you told him the moment I walked in the door. Could you even see me around that donut? Also, if he was expecting me, then why would you have to see if they're ready for me?"

Bimbo number sixteen just looked confused, and before she could blow a fuse and have a total fake blond hair and big boob job meltdown, Maddy said "Never mind."

A couple of minutes later she was ushered into the massive office. When Mr. Schaller stood to greet her, his hand extended and a smile on his face, she stopped, suddenly leery of him. She stared from his hand to the smile as if he was some pod person or she might catch something from him. Trusting this man was not high on her priority list of the things to do.

"Miss Harm, I'm so glad that you are feeling better this morning. I was so glad to hear that you are better from the dreadful car accident." Sincerity nearly dripped from his mouth.

"Oh? Well, maybe you could tell me what you heard, because I wasn't in an accident, car or otherwise. If, however you are referring to these bruises, then you need to ask your boot licker Button about it. He hit me Thursday, and then the abusive prick left me there on the floor covered in blood."

She didn't know why she was called in here, but this couldn't possibly bode well for her. And if she was going down, she was taking as many bodies down with her as she could. Fuck'em all.

"You told me that she was in an accident, and that you had seen to her personally. So what was it Schaller? Was Miss Harm in an accident or did your…boot licker as she called him hit her?" She knew that voice, but the cold steel of anger was new and thankfully not directed at her. She closed her eyes for a second, and then opened them quickly when she heard the chairs.

He was standing now and Mr. MacManus and two other men were as well.

"Could this week get any worse?" She'd said it under her breath, barely moving the air around her mouth, but apparently loud enough for the four men standing there to hear. She glared at them, one and all. "GQ just move into this office, or what? One man looking this good is, well doable, two, okay, but four? I'm still asleep aren't I? I've fallen into a fourth dimension where all the men are gorgeous and I'm…well I'm me. Not you Mr. Shitface, err Schaller, just these guys." She noticed that they were staring at her...oddly even for her. "I'm not asleep am I? You can actually hear me?"

"No, you're not, and yes, we can. Come have a seat Ms. Harm. We've set this meeting up to see if we can all come to a mutual agreement of sorts. This concerns you working for us on a full time basis."

Maddy looked at all five men sitting around the table. She could almost feel the anger emanating from her boss behind her. There was anger from the others as well, but she couldn't figure out what she'd done to piss them off...well, expect for Kyle. She was so going to pay for this, she just knew it. If not from her boss then surely the men sitting here.

Kyle was glaring at the man behind the desk, glared so hard that Sherman began to pull at the collar of his three hundred dollar shirt and two hundred dollar tie. They looked like shit on him anyway, Maddy thought. He stopped glaring long enough to look to where Aaron was leading her over to the conference table and moved to follow them. When she stopped suddenly, he bumped into her from behind. Her whole body tightened. If the chair that Aaron was holding out for her hadn't been there she would have fell to the floor.

"I...no, I don't know...what's this all about Mr. MacManus? I have a right to know what's going on, especially now, with him here." She was pointing at Mr. Schaller. She actually had no idea why any of them were there, especially her.

When Schaller charged forward, Maddy cowered back. She hurt too much to let someone take another swipe at her and she wasn't sure she could take much more. With his hand drawn back in a fist, Schaller snapped out at her.

"This is my office you stupid bit..."

"I wouldn't even *think* the end of that word if I were you. Not if you value your balls where they are." Kyle was at his throat in a second having flashed across the room the moment drew back to hit her. She could only blink in surprise.

Chapter Seven

"That's enough! Perhaps we can all have a seat. Mr...Kyle whatever your name is, sit. Right here, let him go and sit down, I said. Mr. MacManus, could you start, you said something about wanting to talk to me. Go on...you, Kyle Person I said, sit down, damn it!"

Someone had to take charge of this meeting or there was gonna be bloodshed Aaron thought. He could tell she was confused. No one had cared how they had treated her before. Aaron thought that was extremely sad. When she glanced at him just as he was pushing Kyle into a chair and saw that he was grinning she cocked her pretty brow at him in question, he just burst out laughing.

'Keep laughing it up bucko and they'll have the men in white jackets after you too soon enough.' She muttered quietly.

"Ah, Ms Harm you are a delight! Maddy I'd like you to meet some very good friends of mine, Bradley Wolff, you've not met, this is Colin Larimore, I believe you and he have talked on the phone, and this is Kyle Dixon, one of my oldest and dearest friends. Everyone this is Madison Harm, Attorney at Law." Aaron couldn't help it, her banter with herself was funny and her taking charge of the violate situation showed she had what it took to be just what they were looking for. Oh yeah, she was perfect.

Mr. Schaller looked pissed still, but he apparently knew when to keep his mouth shut. Aaron would need to keep a tight rein on Kyle or he'd drain the bastard in a heartbeat. Not that Aaron could blame him, but if Schaller went down it was going to be of his own making.

"Simply put, we would like to hire Ms. Harm as our lawyer, starting as soon as her contract with you can either be bought out or it ends, which ever comes sooner."

Aaron had always believed in the straight forward approach and didn't see any reason to change that because he was working with a human. Well as human as one could consider a 'prick' as Maddy called Sherman Schaller.

"Her contract isn't for sale, nor is it even close to being over," Schaller said in a voice that was meant to end this discussion. "I'm afraid that you have wasted your time gentlemen. Perhaps you'd like to see what, as a firm, we have to offer you. I'm afraid that's the best I can do. I'm sure we have something affordable in your price range. We generally cater to a more…well a different type of clientele than your average customer. What would you say to letting Miss Harm get on with her duties and I have my secretary set you up with one of our more experienced attorney's one of our less busy ones.

"He's right, and at the rate things are going, I'll be working for them until I'm as old as this friggin building." Maddy stood to get some water for the men, and looked startled when all four of them stood as well. Mr. Schaller stood too, but only after a pointed look and a couple of glares from them. She shooed them down and continued speaking. "My original contact was for two years, with an option to renew at anytime. That was four years, three months and twenty seven days ago, but who's counting. Anyway, they didn't tell me that they could renew it without my knowledge or consent. So now I'm up to—"

"They don't need to know the personal business of this firm Ms Harm, nor do I appreciate you airing our business practices out for the public to know." The anger from the man at the head of the table tripled. Aaron knew the other men felt it too. A quick touch of Schaller's mind showed he was going to hurt her and he thought the smack that Robert gave her look like a love tap when he was done with the 'little cunt' he'd called her.

"I want to know. In fact I demand to know. Now," Bradley demanded in a command that had Maddy tremble. But she needn't fear. Bradley liked her.

When Bradley turned to Schaller everyone felt the touch of magic. Only those across from him, Kyle and himself could see what he'd done. He'd dropped a little of his humanity. Just enough to have his canines drop slightly and his eyes to yellow with rage. Bradley Wolfe didn't just become Alpha of the largest pack of 'were's because he was the next in line, he was Alpha because he was one mean ass mother fucker.

"I…you can't. You…you changed. You're eyes…" Sherman sputtered and stood and the smell of fear spiced the air. Sweat appeared on his forehead and beaded on his cheek. Aaron simply smiled at him.

"What is wrong with you" Maddy shouted at her boss. "Do you need a doctor? Mr. Schaller! Pay attention, what is wrong with you? You look like you've seen a ghost."

Maddy had been looking at Sherman and had missed Bradley's show, all she saw was Sherman going deathly white and sliding away from the table so quickly, he nearly knocked the credenza over. Aaron laughed when Bradley mumbled "or maybe a wolf" and smiled showing more teeth than necessary.

"Behave you overgrown pup," Aaron admonished the man. "Maddy why don't you tell us, your boss seems to have lost his ability to speak."

Aaron tapped Bradley none too gently on the arm when he had barked at the man. He was about to lose his ability to hold onto his laughter. He didn't know what had gotten into the wolf, but he wished he take it down a notch or two. Aaron glanced at Colin and saw that he too was getting a kick out of the play, but he had given up all pretexts of trying to look professional. Colin was laughing so hard, tears were streaming down his face.

"Ms. Harm?"

"Yeah, okay. I…I started working…Is he all right? He looks to be in some sort of…I don't know fit or something." She was looking at Colin and keeping an eye on Sherman as well.

However innocent her comment was meant to be, it pushed poor Colin over the edge. He burst out with a laugh so sudden and so loud Maddy jumped in response. Colin had always had a good sense of humor, but for some reason this whole situation had caught him off guard. He got up from his seat and left the room, his loud infectious laughter echoing throughout the room. Maddy looked to first Aaron then both Kyle and Bradley, wondering Aaron was sure what the hell was going on.

"And you people think I'm nuts" she said to no one in particular. Though it was said low, all three of the men left with her heard it. Shaking with barely suppressed mirth, Aaron waved her to continue.

"I graduated from law school at the age of twenty. I wanted to stay local and didn't want to work for one of the larger firms so the choices I had weren't too great. Schaller and Schaller offered to 'help' me pay off my student loans in exchange for two years of servitude then I'd get an increase in pay based on my firm's billable hours. Problem was, they didn't help me with the loan so much as destitute me and I never got to bank any hours for them. No matter how hard I worked, the deeper I got in. Then there is the option. I'm now up to about nine years with this friggin place. Everytime I don't jump when they say, they add time onto my sentence. I've just come to realize I don't want to jump anymore."

"Ah, that explains the comment you made at my house the other week. Yes, I see now." Aaron looked to the head of the table and was surprised to see the man looking smug again. He reached out and captured his thoughts.

"Does she really think this is going to help her, the fucking piece of shit. When we're done here today I will own her ass, maybe even add my own little option of fucking her over the desk clause. That'll teach her a lesson, maybe then she'll see reason. Bitch!" Aaron pulled out of his thoughts, and decided that enough was enough. She was finished working for this firm.

"How did they make you destitute?" Kyle asked and from his tense body, Aaron could tell he had listened in as well.

"Huh, oh, they take twenty five percent of my check and pay it to the bank. It's all legal," she explained quickly a sadness colored her words.

"Damn right it's legal. We pride ourselves on our outstanding record and our law abiding employees. We are a great firm, older than any other around here." Sherman's nose went up in the air. "Gentlemen, as enlightening as this has all been, I believe that I have told you all you needed to hear. Ms. Harm will not be leaving this firm, or she will be in breach of contract, and as for you buying her out, come now, we all know that is just a fairy tale. Banks require money not some pipe dream set forth by four men wanting to get a free, and although I'm sure what is a fine piece of ass." He stood and walked over to the door and opened it, fully expecting them to slink out with their tails between their legs.

"Bradley, I want you to take Maddy out. Take her back to the mansion." The steel in Aaron's voice was cold and hard, and brooked no arguing. "The rest of us need to have a...need to set a few things right for Mr. Schaller."

"I'm not going anywhere. I have to work, this is my job." She was fighting against the hold Bradley had on her arm. But his grip was hard as Aaron knew. "Let me go, or so help me, I'll hurt you."

Bradley just grinned at her, and kept moving her toward the door. In a blur of movement and bright colors he was across the room, untangling himself from Kyle and Aaron. Colin was just picking himself up from the wall where he was sitting too. She had physically thrown a full grown wolf into three other men.

"I told them to stop, but did they listen, oh no, that'd be too easy. Stupid hardheaded men. Why do they do it, piss a woman off? It's because they think we're small and helpless, mindless twits.' She was pacing, back and forth in front of them, and of course, talking to herself. With a snarl she turned on Kyle.

"Is that what you think? I'm mindless? Well, I'll have you know I have a perfectly good brain, well most of the time. And I'm not the least bit helpless. I've taken classes; I was at the head of my self defense class. I'm strong!"

"I can see that. You can handle yourself quite..." Kyle started, pride evident in his voice. But Maddy wasn't having any of it.

"Don't you dare talk down to me, you Neanderthal. I'll toss you again if you're not careful."

She gathered up her jacket and things, and as much dignity as she could scrape together and left the office. When Kyle started to follow her she turned on him quickly. Aaron would have been impressed if he could have stopped laughing long enough.

"I have a gun, and I'm not afraid to use it." She turned to him then and brushed at the tears streaming down her cheeks. Aaron immediately felt contrite as she left the office.

Chapter Eight

"I need to talk to you, privately." Kyle moved further into the room and closed the door behind him. He thumbed the lock shut as he leaned back against the door.

"I don't wanna talk with you anymore. I have a headache and I want to get to work. Go away. I don't like you today."

He could hear the hurt in her voice and knew that he'd caused it. He and he alone was responsible for most of the hurt and pain she'd endured over the past few days and he wanted…no he needed to make it up to her. He looked around at the room she was in. He thought he'd seen better dungeons in his lifetime.

"You have to come with me Madison; I can't stay out much more today. I've about hit the limit now. I'm going to take you back to Aaron's with me and we are going to talk. Okay?" He was walking toward her slowly, carefully. He believed her about the gun, after she had pulled that defense move on them upstairs he had no doubt that she was capable of taking care of herself.

"See, you say that as if I have a choice, or that you plan to give me one. And I can tell that you *think* that you are gonna do just what you say you're going to. As I've said, I have no intentions of going anywhere with you, I have work to do. Now, Mr. Dixon, I'd like for you to leave."

He was close now very close he could almost feel her heat. She stiffened when he leaned down, his breath blowing across the little hairs at her nape that moved with each of her breaths. Her sigh then her moan moved over him, through him. He touched her shoulder with his mouth and placed an open mouth kiss there that gave him a taste of her warm skin.

"I need you Madison. It's time for us to…past time for us to leave," he whispered in her mind.

He felt her response to him, smelled her arousal, the flavor that was hers and hers alone. Touching her made his cock hard, his pulse speed up. He felt the ache of his fangs as they stretched in his gums. Need for her, a need to taste her, to mark her made him want desperately to press her against the table where she sat and take her. *"I want you. I want you to come with me." H*e ran his fingers down her bare arm, his voice caressing her, seducing her. *"Sleep, love. Sleep"*

~~~

She woke with a start. Her body was on fire with…with need? No, that couldn't be right; she didn't need anything, or anyone. She moved on the big bed and…*bed*!

Her eyes popped open and she stiffened. There was someone in the bed with her, someone big. She couldn't see a damned thing as the room was a black as pitch, but getting up seemed imperative. She moved to what she hoped was the side of the bed and stopped again. She was, groaned, she was naked

"Ooookkkk," she said out loud. "Think, Maddy, think. Okay, this isn't as bad as it seems. Well, okay that was a lie. This is pretty fucked up girl. You're in a strange bed, naked in the dark, there seems to be a large…hummm thing, no we are not calling it a body, it's a thing. Focus," she told herself. "There is a large something lying next to you...I wonder if it's naked too. Damn it Madison Shelby Harm you have to stay with me. We are..."

"Yes. To both actually, I'm a body, and I am quite naked. I find I sleep better in the raw, nothing to restrict you if you have a...need." Kyle rolled over on top of her and she felt his heat and knew that all that separated them was the blanket. "If you're done with your assessment of the situation, I can fill you in with the rest."

"Did we...I mean have we...are you...did we have sex?"

She had always thought that sex was a stupid pastime, messy and sloppy. She hated to think that it happened without her knowledge, though. Losing one's virginity should be something a person should be awake for, she thought. At least that seemed reasonable to her.

Kyle rolled over and covered her with is body. He pressed down on her with his hips, making her very aware, even through the covers that he was erect and hard. He pulled her hands above her head, lacing his fingers through hers and nuzzled her neck, nipping at her. He moved up to her ear and with a little bite, whispered to her.

"When we make love Madison, you will be wide awake and most assuredly know that it's happening."

He sucked her lower lip into his mouth and groaned. Moving both her hands into one of his, he brought his free hand down to her face and tilted her head. He looked into her eyes, and brushed his lips across hers.

"Madison..." he groaned her name.

His mouth was hot, demanding, and hard, his tongue swept along hers in a duel, a dance. She wanted to touch him, to pull him closer, her fingers gripped at his hand, trying to convey her need to him, but he wouldn't listen, or didn't want to. When he pulled his mouth from hers, tore it really, he was breathing as hard, no panting as hard as she was, his need her need mingling together.

"Please?" She whimpered to him, not really sure what she wanted, but knew without a doubt that he was the one who could give it to her.

As soon as her hands were free, she wrapped them into his silky hair, pulled him down to her mouth again. When he pushed the blankets down and her breast was exposed she nearly came off the bed when he touched her, his groan vibrating through her breast and to her core. Slowly, slowly he leaned down, watching her as he moved toward her, her nipple straining to greet him, her body arching to meet him. When his tongue rasped against the hard peak, then suckled it into his mouth, she cried out. Maddy pulled him tighter to her even as he pulled more of the fleshy flesh deeper into his mouth, sucking hard. He moved to free the other breast, pulling and tugging on the blanket, then suckled the other hardened nipple. Back and forth he went, first one then the other, nipping on them then lathing them with his hot wet mouth. She was on fire.

She felt him stiffen, his entire body tense for several seconds before she realized that there was a pounding, not of her heart as she had thought, but on the door, someone was pounding on the door. He turned then and snarled something, she wasn't sure what but in a language she'd never heard before. But it didn't stop. Whoever it was, they kept beating and yelling back to him in the same language. He looked back at her, even in the dark she could see that his eyes were dark, but he was already pulling away, both physically and sensually.

~~~

Kyle rolled to his back and tried his best to calm his body and mind. *Fuck! He*'d nearly taken her, made love to her when they were all waiting for them. Aaron told him that he needed to wait, to explain. She had no idea what they were and it was time to explain. Kyle wanted to bring her back to him, pull her into his arms, but he knew that they would not be leaving this bedroom if he did.

When she made to get up, he reached for her. She jerked hard away at his touch, turned on the bedside lamp and stood before him, naked. He'd never seen all of her body before. If he'd thought his body on fire before seeing her like this nearly killed him.

"Madison, you're—"

"I want my clothes. Where are they?" She walked over to the wingback chair that sat near the now cold fireplace. She picked up the two articles of clothing that belonged to him, and seeing that, she tossed them back into the chair. When she turned and looked at him expectantly, he couldn't remember what she had said. "My clothes, where are they?"

Kyle could only point and hoped that he was giving her whatever she seemed to be asking him for. There was no blood in his head, at least not the one above his shoulders. When she turned toward the bathroom and walked away, he groaned. Her backside was better than the front, if that was even possible. Fuck he was hard and hurting. When the bathroom door closed with a click and the telltale sound of the lock turning registered he sat up, and before he knew it he was at the door where she was. The shower turned on before he could think to make his tongue wrap around a word to talk to her. What he might have said, he didn't have a clue, but he knew three things: a, she was by far the most beautiful woman he'd ever seen, b, he wanted her with every fiber of his being and c, she was madder than hell at him and he didn't have the slightest idea why.

Chapter Nine

Shower, wash, dry, dress, leave. Shower, wash, dry, dress, leave. These five words had been running through her head since she had gotten out of his bed. She had accomplished one and was working number two pretty good. The tears streaming down her face were easy enough to ignore while the water was running, but she figured she'd have to deal with them as soon as she got to number three.

"Well, I'll deal with that when I get there, no since buying trouble. He didn't want me again. Nope, not going there, I have three more words to get through first."

Rinsing her hair she began to make progress to number three and the drying issue that was sure to arise. Turning off the shower proved to be a little tricky. Her eyes seemed to have decided to blur up in addition to leak all over the place, but she finally managed to get it off and leaned against the wall to try and get up the energy to move on with her list. There was a big fluffy towel hanging over a warming rack all nice and toasty for her.

She meticulously dried herself and used another towel to dry her hair. When she decided she'd delayed the process long enough she pulled her clothes to her and sighed. The tears started to fall again.

She pulled her dress pants on without her panties. She was not putting her dirty under clothes back on and the bra and camisole went next. She was just pulling the comb she'd found in the drawer through her hair when she heard 'him' in the other room.

"He is no longer anyone I'm going to concern myself with. Now," she said to herself. "In order to finish my list, I just need to open the door and walk out. You can open the door. You do it all the time. Just turn the knob, good girl and push open the wooden thing." Taking a deep breath she walked thought the door way.

~~~

When she walked past him with her nose in the air, Kyle knew he was in serious trouble. Her eyes and nose were red and she wouldn't look at him. Yeah, he was a dead man, time to grovel, he thought.

"Madison, I'm so sorr—" She turned suddenly, and advanced on him quickly backing him up against the wall behind him. He could feel the blaze of her anger and his cock hardened with her scent.

"If you fucking tell me you're sorry again, I will hurt you." Her eyes were bright, the blue darkened to almost black.

They stood staring at each other for several tense filled seconds until she turned her back on him and went to the door. He leaned hard against the wall she had backed him to and closed his eyes. He wasn't sure what to think, but he knew without a doubt he'd done something to really piss her off. And he couldn't help but smile.

Aaron and Sara were sitting on the couch and Bradley and the children were there as well. Kyle took a seat in one of the wingback chairs near the fireplace and sat. He wanted to pace more than anything in the world but as everyone else was sitting he would as well.

Kyle decided that he really liked this room. It was homey and warm, yet extremely functional. When the furniture was moved out and into storage it was just a long room without any character. But when it was in use as is was now as a simple living room, it was comfy. There were four full sized gray and pink couches that circled around a large fireplace and hearth. The grate that sat in the firebox was as big as a full sized bed and could easily burn a core of wood without any problems. The stone mantle was made up of pink and gray marbled quartz and had a slab of the same material as the base. Along both sides of it were large floor to ceiling windows that looked out over the back of the property that was mostly woods. Sliding doors that lead out onto a covered patio and pool completed the wall. Bookshelves covered the other walls, with chairs scattered about in pairs filling out the rest of the room. Madison was sitting in one of the only chairs in the circle of couches.

"I'm glad everyone could finally join us." Aaron looked pointedly at Kyle. He simply shrugged at him. He had more important things to contend with just now than making people wait for him to being a meeting. Aaron continued. "Maddy. I want to first say how sorry I am about this morning. It could have gone much smoother and I'm afraid we may have inadvertently caused you more problems than we meant to. If you don't mind, we'll take this up—"

"I want to leave please. I don't know how I got here, and frankly I don't care, but I want to leave." She stood and the men of the room did as well. When she moved toward the door Kyle intercepted her. He didn't touch her but he wasn't about to let her leave until this was finished.

"Madison, you need to sit down. We have something to tell you. Things you need to know so that we can move on as a business."

He, they all needed to tell her what they were. It had gotten to the point where she needed to be made aware of their being non-human.

"And I want you to fuck off." She rubbed her forehead and lowered her voice. "If you do not move your big arrogant obnoxious ass out of my way, I swear I will. I've had enough." She crossed her arms over her chest and began tapping her foot as if she actually expected him to move.

"Maddy, I need to talk to you please. It's really, really, really important. I gots a message for you." Kyle looked down at Mac, Aaron's son. Now was not the time. Kyle needed to have this conversation with her.

"I'm sorry Mr. and Mrs. MacManus," Maddy flushed a deep red. "I should have stopped to think before speaking. What kind of message do you have for me Mac?" Maddy knelt down on her knees to look at the young boy. She looked at little Mac like Kyle wished she'd look at him, if only just once.

"I'm a naked dancer and I gots to give you a message from your gram—", he rushed on to tell her. Kyle looked at Aaron. It was the look of concern on his face that caused Kyle to pause.

"You're a necromancer you baboon, not a naked dancer. How stupid can you be? Naked dancer—She probably thinks you dance in the grass like a silly witch." Lizzy shook her head as she made fun of her brother.

"Elizabeth MacManus don't call your brother names. It's very rude. What kind of message do you have for Maddy, son?" Kyle could see that Aaron was trying to be stern with his daughter and not laugh at his son. Kyle thought it was hilarious but didn't laugh either. He wouldn't hurt the kid for anything.

"As I was telling her before somebody had to make fun of me, it's from your Grammie. She wants me to telled you something.

Something she forgot." He cocked his head at Maddy, a concerned look on his face. "It's okay. I know how to put her back. She just came to me to tell you this."

"I...that's not funny Mac. Who put you up to this? You should...My Grammie is dead, you can't of...Necromancers aren't real. I...she's dead." Maddy looked around the room. Kyle supposed she was looking for help, thinking no one in the room would believe him either.

"It's okay Maddy" Lizzy said trying to be helpful. "He talks to ghosts all the time. It's 'cause he was almost dead when Aunt Pic birthed us. He is learning to put 'em back okay. Don't be mad." Lizzy patted Maddy on the back. Kyle had a feeling this was not helping at all.

"You believe him. You shouldn't encourage him to...there are no such things as...I have to go." Maddy started to rise to leave. Kyle could tell she'd had too much. But there was no turning back now.

"Of course there are, Maddy. Just like there are vampires, werewolves and other creatures that go bump in the night. Just like we are." Kyle looked over at his best friend and decided that murder might be worth the console being pissed at him.

"You are?" Her voice was weak and tight, her eyes were wide and her pupils dilated. They all could hear her heart pounding with terror as well as he did, her breaths short and harsh.

"Yes, love, we all are. With the exception of Bradley over there who's an alpha 'were, we're all vamps. Some of us are a little extra. Like for instances, Sara and Lizzy are also magical beings, related to the Queen of all Magic." Kyle stood slowly and moved toward her, knowing she was close to losing it. This could have gone a good deal better. He nodded to Aaron, but could see that he'd already saw the situation could go bad. Kyle moved to a little closer to her.

"Of course, why not. If you're going to believe your vampires, why the heck not have a queen too. I can't breathe, I need to breathe." She ran toward the glass door and it opened before she could get to it. She stopped so suddenly that Kyle who had made to follow her bumped into her back. "Don't touch me! You all need help serious help. I...I'm leaving. I...you people are sick."

"Madison, calm down. Let us explain." Kyle and Aaron were closing in on her. Kyle knew that if she left here she could hurt herself. She wasn't thinking and that could put her in harms way.

"Calm down? Calm down? Are you fucking insane. You just told me that you're all vampires and you want me to calm down. Well, *fuck off*." She darted to the kitchen area.

Chapter Ten

Duncan was putting food – little cakes, cookies and a slice of pie on a large tray. She noticed that there were cups and glasses there as well. This was all too surreal for her and she sat down hard on a chair.

"They eat? I mean, they eat food? There's always food here when I come, they can't be vampires and eat, can they?" She knew she was babbling, but couldn't seem to stop herself. It was that or start screaming and tearing at her hair.

"Ah, they have told you. No, Miss, the gentlemen do not eat food. The ladies all eat however and the little ones of course. We are not sure why the ladies can partake of food, but there you have it."

"Yes, there I have it. I need to use the phone, I…I'm going home you see and I need to leave." She put her hand over her pounding heart. "There are things going on that I don't…can't understand. I need to go home and have someone wake me up. Yes, that's it. I'm asleep." Duncan shook his head and she didn't ask him what he meant. She was actually very afraid he'd give her and answer she didn't want to hear.

"Of course Miss, but I can transport you. It would be my pleasure." He took off his pristine white apron. Then he reached over and took his coat off the rack near the door. He had just picked up a set of keys when the door behind her opened. She didn't turn around.

She knew that Sara was there, could feel her eyes burrowing into her, but she refused to look at her. Maddy just stood at the opposite side of the room, her back to the room and faced the outer door.

"Maddy," Sara asked quietly. "Are you all right?"

"Yes, Mr. Duncan, I'd like it if you could take me home. I seemed to have lost my...my car. I could use a ride. Please, right now. I need to leave right now."

Maddy didn't want to hear what Sara had to say so she kept talking about the ride home and her car and anything else that popped into her mind until Duncan led her out the door and to the garage.

Maddy didn't say a word once they got into the big Hummer and she had given Duncan an address. She had just moved over to the window and huddled against the glass staring out of the rain streaked covered window. Her mind was just overwhelmed.

Maddy was thinking hard, her heart and her head hurt. Vampires and werewolves, and the little boy believed he was a necromancer. Magic, there was something about magic she was suppose to remember, but couldn't. Kyle had pushed her away twice. Blood and food. Nothing was making sense, yet everything was swirling around and around. She realized that they had been stopped for a while and looked to see where they were. In front of not her home, but a place that should have been—the house of their dreams, her and her grandmother's dreams.

"We were going to buy this house, my Grammie and me. She was going to take art classes and I was going to practice law out the back. There's a little garden in the corner that had daffodils when we were here to look at it. Aren't they the happiest flower?"

She looked for a few more minutes, Duncan not saying a word. "They really are vampires aren't they Mr. Duncan, and that little boy Mac, he spoke to her, my Grammie, didn't he?"

"Yes, Miss." He didn't elaborate. She wasn't sure what else he could say to her. She was certain she might be having a breakdown of some sort and was sure once someone gave her something stronger everything would be fine. Then again...

"Yeah, of course they are." She closed her eyes before she spoke again. "I don't live here. I'm not even sure why I had you bring me here. My mind seems to be a little befuddled."

Maddy was quite for a long while thinking, and then came to a decision.

"Would you tell Mr. MacManus that I'll work for him, I really don't have a choice really. But I have rules that I'll discuss with him when he can see me." She opened the door and got out. It started raining then; the skies seem to open up and drenched her. "I don't have a phone, but there's a pay phone on the floor where I stay." She reached in again for a piece of notepaper that was in the cars tray and a pen. She wrote the number down and gave it to Duncan.

"Miss, you cannot stay out here. Come. Return to the vehicle and get in and let me dispatch you to your home." Duncan started to get out of the car but she back away and shut the door.

"It's all right Mr. Duncan. I don't have a key to get in to my home anyway. It's still in my bag at the office. I hope so anyway. And staying in a hotel is out, I don't have the money for that, and I have no ID anyway. I need to think, I'm just gonna walk around for awhile. Don't worry about me." She slammed the door and took off in the pouring rain before he could argue with her more.

~~~

"Master Kyle, you left her things at that office. Now she is running around in the dark without a proper place to sleep tonight. What were you thinking?" Duncan hadn't even waited to remove his rain slicker before confronting Kyle.

"What do you mean, she's running around? You left her outside in this? Why the hell didn't you take her ho—" Kyle stood up to...

He actually wasn't sure what he was going to do but sitting put him at a disadvantage to the little man. But he didn't think all the height in the world would make him any bigger in the man in front of him.

"You will not blame me for this mess. I did not bring her into this house without her things; I did not upset her to the point of tears! You did," Duncan yelled at him. "Now you will listen to me. You will not make her cry again. Or you will be answering to me. Do I make myself understood? I was a boxing champ in my day and I'll not hesitate to pop you a knuckle sub if you get out of line again." Duncan shook his fist at Kyle again and went into the kitchen. He had never seen him look so angry in his life, Kyle thought.

Kyle didn't know whether to laugh or beg forgiveness. He turned to look at the rest of the occupants of the room and every one of them stood staring open-mouthed at the door Duncan had just exited.

"I'm guessing he's never threatened anyone with a knuckle sub before."

Chapter Eleven

"City morgue, you stab 'em, we slab 'em." The voice at the other end of the phone was decidedly female, but slurred. Aaron wasn't sure if he had the right number or not and checked again to be sure. Yes, it was the correct one.

"Yes. Yes, I would like to speak to a Madison Harm please. Do you think that you could find her for me?" Surely she wouldn't have given them the number to the morgue as a joke.

"Yeah, I think. Hang on. Is the Mad Hatter here? Hey," he shouted nearly bursting Aaron's ear drum. "Anyone seen the Mad Hatter today? Hang on buddy, if she's here, somebody will get her for you." The phone was set down on something metal, more than likely the top of the pay phone was Aaron's guess.

The *Mad Hatter*, huh? Aaron wondered at that. The 'mad' part he got, from Madison no doubt, and then with the way the phone had been answered, he figured out the rest from the madness of the people in the building.

Aaron waited three minutes before she came on the line. While waiting for her he over heard a profusion of conversations as people walked by the open line. They ranged from a drug deal going down to someone who needed to let her 'hang-buddy' know she was late again.

"This is Madison Harm. May I help you?"

To Aaron she sounded resigned, beaten. He thought he liked her better fighting and spitting.

"Ms Harm, its Aaron MacManus. I called to see if you could come by the estate tonight. We have a great deal to discuss, one of which will be your living arrangement. That place isn't safe for a young woman as I'm sure you are aware. And bring a few changes of clothing, as it will be late when we finish and it will take a few days I believe to get things settled to my satisfaction."

Aaron was used to getting his own way and didn't think anything of setting up the arrangements for her to suit himself. Besides, he had her best interest at heart and he really wanted to piss her off again.

"I see. I can't come over this evening, I have a prior commitment. And as for your arrangements, let me say first of all, I won't be spending the night or any night, but thanks for asking. Secondly, my living arrangements are none of your business and lastly, we'll settle things to both of our satisfactions or not at all. I'm not a pushover Mr. MacManus, and the sooner you figure that out the better things will go for all of us." Maddy's voice had picked up with her temper he thought, and she sounded less broken as well.

He burst out laughing. She had fire and spirit, he'd give her that. And he liked a good fight as well as the next man. But he knew he'd win.

"Ah, Ms Harm, I think we are going to suit well working together, very well indeed. I'll see you tomorrow night then."

~~~

"I need six draft, three 7&7 and a Harvey. I'm so glad you're here through the week now Mad." Shelly told her.

Shelly Jones, wife to the bars owner, worked and was co owner, at the bar, *Puss n' Boots* three nights a week and all day on

Saturday when a game was playing. Maddy usually only worked Friday nights to help out as an extra bartender and could according to Shelly serve up drinks faster than anyone she'd ever seen. Maddy thought it was because Tina, the usual bartender was slower than molasses.

"Thanks Shell. I'm just glad Paul could use me. I don't know what I would have done without his help and the extra hours right now. I should be thanking you guys."

Maddy worked on the mixed drinks first, and poured the bourbon chaser for the Harvey at the same time. Fisting three mugs at a time she began building the drafts, it took someone a lot of time to get the proportions of a draft right, too much head wasn't right and too little would get you thrown out of this bar.

Puss n' Boots wasn't a bar families came into. It was more a bar you went to get drunk and have a fist fight in the parking lot you might have just puked your guts up into. Then there were the strippers. Maddy had been working part-time there since the week she'd turn twenty one. Paul, Shelly's husband owned the bar and had hired Maddy not because he thought she was a great bartender, but because she was 'drop dead gorgeous and built like a brick shit house', whatever that meant. Maddy was just happy for the work.

At first she'd been a little uncomfortable working there at nights alone, but Paul had lent her his Equalizer, his Glock forty and showed her how to use it, and since then she'd felt much better. And after the third time she had to pull it and the second time she'd used it, the patrons knew that though she was a pretty little thing, don't fuck with her. She never concealed it, but carried it right on her left hip were there was no doubt that she was armed. There was also three Louisville sluggers at different intervals under the bar if things got a little too close for comfort.

It was nearly four-thirty in the morning when she went out to her car to leave. Her feet ached and her lower back was killing her. But she'd made a hundred and sixty-four dollars in tips plus Jake had made her a burger and fries for dinner. A couple more nights like this and she'd be able to get four used tires instead of two, plus be able to catch up on her rent. She thanked Jake, the cook for walking her to her car and drove home.

She'd been purposely not thinking about the interview at the MacManus place tomorrow…no, well tonight now. But now that she wasn't busy anymore and just laying in her single bed it came crashing in again. Vampires. Werewolves too. She wasn't sure what to think about it, so she tried not to. She didn't want to have to be there after sunset, and she knew that she needed to avoid Master Kyle as much as possible. She wasn't sure what her job would entail, but she was reasonably sure it would need to be done during the daylight hours, so that took care of the sunset deadline. Also by the same logic, working with the sun out would keep her away from Kyle. She figured she had a win-win situation. She hoped.

The sun was well into the sky by the time she fell asleep, and almost two o'clock in the afternoon when the nightmare started.

"Hello my dear, what'sss taken you ssso long to visssit me?" The voice was deep, and sounded hissed rather than spoken. The sound of it, low and full of anger making the hair on the back of her neck stand up and stiffen.

"Who are you? Where am I?" Maddy looked around the…area. It wasn't a room, she was sure of that, but a void. There was no color here, just white and the air felt, not heavy really but old. It was like a room shut up for a very long time, allowing no air exchange.

"Why, you've come to me, to your home. I've been waiting, yesss, yesss I have. You ssshould not have gone. No, no not gone from me. I have plansss for you. Plansss for you and me. We will be together for all timesss. You musst come to me. "

He or it sounded as though it was male. She didn't know why she thought that but it felt right.

"I asked you a question. Where am I? What do you mean I'm home? I make my own plans, my life belongs to me and no one else, Understand me? This isn't my home, I don't know who you are and I demand that—"

She felt its anger hit her less than a second later. It scorched over her skin like a live flame, burning her flesh and hurting to the point of her wanting to scream.

"You will demand nothing. I will make demands. I will be obeyed. I am lord and master. You are mine and the sooner you remember that the better things will go for you. You're an ungrateful bitch."

It screamed through her head even as she woke up. The sound felt as though it was tearing its way into her memory, into her brain. The scream was just dying on her lips when she realized that someone was pounding on her door and yelling at her to open up.

Heart still pounding and head hurting, Maddy stumbled her way to her door. Taking off the two chains and thumbing the deadbolt took some work because she just couldn't get her mind to work around making her body work. When it finally opened Marcie from down the hall tumbled in.

"Oh god girlfriend, are you ok? I mean that was some wicket screaming you was a piping out there. Scared the shits right outta me and Frank, and we was right in the middle of doing the nasty. Oh girl you look like a dead cat, maybe you should, I don't know take a couple of pills and chill awhile. I gots me some downer's I can share witch ya. No charge, you know what I mean? You my homey." Sometimes, like right now, Maddy felt as if she needed a translator when talking with Marcie.

She was an odd girl to begin with, but seeing her made her oddity seem normal for her. Marcie's hair was bright, bright green with varying strips of neon colors throughout it. Her clothes, when she was wearing any, thank goodness now was one of those times, were a mishmash of dots and stripes, plaids and patch. She tended to carry an extra thirty pounds of munchies weight and did more coke than any three people Maddy knew.

"No thanks, but I do think I'll go take a shower. Tell Frank I said I was sorry for interr…for umm, well tell Frank I'm sorry."

Maddy felt her face heat up. It's not that she meant to, but a sudden picture of Frank and Marcie doing the nasty filtered through her head at that moment and she felt embarrassed and slightly sick.

Maddy gathered up her cleaning supplies, toiletries and clothes and shuffled down to the shower. She always cleaned the shower stall before she entered it, sharing a bathroom with ten other people wasn't the most sanitary place on earth. Then she stripped down and stepped under the hot spray. When she reached her hands up over her head to wash then rinse her hair she felt a tightening in her left shoulder. She thought she must have pulled something moving that keg to the back, she thought.

"Stupid girl, whatcha thinking moving something that weighs that much without help, you trying to kill you?' She smiled. She hadn't spoken to herself in a couple of days and was beginning to believe she might be sane, "can't have that now can we?"

By the time she was dressed and had cleaned up her bed, nightmares had a messy aftermath on sheets it seemed, and ate it was nearly six o'clock in the evening. She decided to go by a fast food restaurant and treat herself to a quick but satisfying dinner before going to…she wasn't sure what this was, but meeting sufficed for now. At seven forty-seven she was pulling into the MacManus driveway. And she'd only had to look at her map twice and only got lost once.

"You go girl," she congratulated herself. Pushing the buzzer with a bright smile, she looked up into the security camera and waved when she hear the mike picked up at the other end.

"Hey Mr. Duncan, it's Madison Harm, I have an appointment at eight o'clock." She was beaming at the camera.

"It's Kyle, Madison, Dunc is busy, but come on up." Her mood went from buoyant to crappy just like that.

"I don't know why he's friggin here, stupid arrogant jerk. Just what I need, another vampire in the mix. Stupid bloodsuckers." She was in a fine snit as she circled the drive in front of the garage.

By the time she was out of her car and had gathered up her things, she had just about convinced herself that her entire bad luck lately was solely his fault. Her vocabulary had improved, exponentially.

"Thank you very much Master Kyle. And you'd better watch your step if you know what's good for you." This might have been delivered a tad too late to herself as she was pretty sure the man in question had heard it.

"I'm sure you'll get a chance to try it out on me throughout the night Miss Madison. You do seem to bring out the best in me." The man was insufferable and a pig and was thinking that someone needed to take him down a peg or two. Well she was just going to ignore him.

She was surprised when he leaned in, it was as if he couldn't help himself; he needed a fix of her, a deep breath of her scent. Leaning in, he nuzzled her neck and inhaled deeply and licked her throat. He pulled back from her with a frown.

"What have you been doing today? Burning dinner?"

What a thing to ask, did he not have one lick of manners.

"You keep your nose to yourself and…and everything else too, and no I haven't been burning dinner. I don't even know how to cook. Burning dinner indeed. What are you doing here anyway, you're leaving soon I hope."

When he had put his face into her shoulder it was everything she could do not to pull his head in tighter. And his tongue, it had taken nearly ounce of her willpower not to let her eyes cross it had felt that good. Wow but the man had sexy down to an art. She turned away from him and headed in the direction he had pointed.

Chapter Twelve

Kyle decided that she was only there to drive him mad. And the sooner she had her meeting the better it would be on his peace of mind.

He could smell her arousal now, it was deep and heady. If he didn't keep her pissed off at him for the rest of the night, there wasn't going to be a meeting, at least not between the five of them, but her and him meeting the silk sheets on his bed he thought.

Kyle had been in a semi erect state since he'd met her, especially after the other night in his bed when she'd gotten up and had walked around his room naked. It was all he could do to make it two hours without having to go and jerk off just thinking about that luscious body of hers, those full breasts, tasty nipples and that ass. Christ, an ass a man could get lost in for hours. And he wanted to, he wanted to bury himself deep in her heat and lose himself. He was hurting, his cock was hard and hurting, and there was no time to take care of it. He wasn't going to make it, with his hard-on and her scent; he just wasn't going to make it. His best defense tonight was to piss her off and piss her off royally.

"Kyle, are you bringing her in here, or should we give you two a few minutes?" Great just what he needed, Aaron tapping into him and his dilemma, and thinking it was funny too.

"Fuck you, you obnoxious prick," he snapped back. *"She's aroused. What am I suppose to do, throw her against the wall and have at it? I would like to think I have better manners than that."* He would hope so too, but now that he'd thought about it, slamming her against the nearest wall did sound good.

"Hummm, I believe Sara and I might have used the pew there in the entrance hall once or twice. You might want to be on the top though; it's not quite wide enough for you. Unless of course she's riding you, then all sorts of possibilities can arise." Aaron was enjoying himself, Kyle could tell. He wanted Kyle to mate with Maddy and soon he'd told him just before she'd gotten there. He'd told him he didn't know why but felt that it was imperative that Kyle did so.

"Jesus, that's an image I could have done without. Your old, naked body writhing around with that delicious piece of fine flesh like my Sara...it must have been a pity fuck."

Maddy, unaware of the sexual banter between Aaron and Kyle walked into the salon just ahead of Kyle. And just as he'd said, there were Colin and Bradley with Mr. MacManus.

"Have a seat Maddy, we're about to become very wealthy."

~~~

"The four of us, Bradley, Kyle, Colin and myself are going into business together and you are going to be our lawyer. We each are going to invest a predetermined dollar amount then buy the buildings and convert them into what we need. It will be a four way split, equal shares equal investments."

The men had been going over plans since they arose and Bradley showed up. Aaron had made notes and was referring to them now as he gave Maddy the barest of bones of what they had discussed.

"Whoa there cowboy. Don't put the horse before the cart. What buildings? The one's on Merchant Way?" Aaron nodded, impressed with her ability to work it out so quickly. "I suppose you could get them cheap enough, provided that no one gets wind of what you're doing. Once word gets out that a group of businessmen are buying up properties in an area, the price could sky rocket. Or worse yet a couple of wanna be entrepreneurs go in and buy one or two and fuck you royal when you need that particular site to finish a project. How many building are you thinking?"

He looked down at his sheet of notes. "How many are there?"

"There are nineteen warehouses and six store fronts. There are also a couple of strip malls, but they need to be torn down. They're all too small and very out of date. Along the outer edge of the area is an apartment building. I think some homeless people have taken over that building. That will need to come down as well, bad investment in the long run trying to get them to move out." Aaron was impressed again by her. She knew not only which buildings were viable to them and which needed to be rehabbed.

"All of them then. We want to keep control of the area and be able to decide what goes in and what doesn't. Is that possible, buying them all I mean?"

Aaron like Bradley thought the purchase of all of the buildings was risky, but smart in the long run and had helped him convince the other two. Now they just needed to bring Maddy on board.

"All…shit all of them!! That'll be twenty to thirty buildings and property. Let's see," Maddy pulled out her lap top and began making notes on a sticky note that was stuck under the key board. "With taxes and asking price alone, you're talking seventy three million. If we could keep this quite until the end, you could probably get them for about forty, fifty million tops. Then the rework on them, which could cost as much if not more…What is it you're planning if you don't mind my asking?"

"You'll need to know," Colin said with a smile. "We'll need permits to open and liquor licenses. We want to open a vampire/were bar."

Colin leaned back in his seat. Now is when Aaron had figured she'd shoot them down. They all had their notes; each one ready with a counter argument to meet with what they were sure would be all in the vein of talking them out of this venture, or at least he hoped they did.

"And the other buildings, they'd be what?" She was stalling, Aaron could tell, she wasn't sure what or even if there was a precedent for this kind of business, but she needed to think before she spoke. Always a good idea as an attorney he figured and liked her even more for not saying the first thing on her mind.

"Several of the warehouses would be converted into apartments, or lairs depending on the needs. The malls, as you said will be demolished. The apartment building we hadn't considered the need to tear it down as well, but I can see your point in that." Aaron made a note on his paper before he continued. "We also thought to add health care facilities, such as medical and long term stay. While our kind heals quickly, the need to recuperate over time is sometimes needed. Also a teaching facility, it's a problem for some of us to blend readily into the human world and a way for us to work with some of the slang and terms would be beneficial." Aaron was thinking of Duncan and his constant misuse of the slang, although it made him seem more human somehow.

"Are you talking total segregation? I don't see how that will work unless you plan to put up a bubble around the area. You'll need to go very main stream if this is what you really want. People, humans as you call us will want to be a part of it just because you didn't want them to. Blood will need to be made readily available, as will medical supplies whatever those might be. No offense, but if you're talking werewolves you'd need to hire a vet, right?"

"No, we are animals but we have specialized doctors as well," Bradley told her with a smile. "And none taken, you're doing very well for someone whose know about us for what, about twenty-four hours. You haven't freaked out once."

Aaron liked that she didn't pull back when she spoke; she was as natural as they came.

"If you stay non-fury, I'll be fine. By the way, the other day at the office, what did you do to Schaller?" They could all hear her nervousness now. "I'm assuming now that you must have scared him somehow, what was it, did you swish your tail or something? I had thought about that in one of my random walks through the whole 'vampire, werewolf, necromancer, oh my' journey's, sung to the tune of that Disney song, you know the one."

"Would you like to see, I've been dying to show you the real me." At her nod, Bradley dropped a little of his humanity. His eyes changed to a deep golden color from the beautiful baby blues and his canines dropped, his jaw elongating slightly. It all took less than two seconds.

"Fuck! Okay, don't do that again. But now that I see it, I can see why he looked like he wanted to shit himself. I should have had you around when the paperboy tried to get frisky, sorry fresh."

"What paperboy? Who is he?" Kyle went from semi comatose looking to jealous rage in less time than it took Bradley to change.

"Back off buck-o, I took care of him. Eventually. All right he's still a bother, but he's only fourteen and I think he'll get over me as soon as the girl next door gets her boobs. Mine will be too passé by then." She tried to sound flippant, but it came off annoyed sounding.

"There is nothing passé about your breasts, they are perfect. I like them very much." Kyle hadn't meant to say anything Aaron thought and rolled his eyes at his friend. The words slipping out before his brain could think about who was in the room with them apparently.

The room grew perfect silent, the tension always there on the surface between them, bloomed to a palatable tangible thing. Aaron was amazed at the amount of sexual tension between the two of them.

"Madison, I'm s…" He started to apologize to her and then stopped suddenly. The look she was giving him made Aaron think she was seriously contemplating taking a silver knife to his throat or better yet to his dick. Aaron was hard pressed not to burst out laughing.

"What do you think, can we pull it off?" Changing the subject and the atmosphere was needed and lame as it was, if this was the best that Colin could come up and do the trick, Aaron would have to remember to thank him later.

"I'll need to get started soon. Hummm…let's see." She rubbed her forehead. "I guess we should talk time frame and such, but I've got to tell you I'm whipped. I can get you some information and drop it off here sometime tomorrow afternoon. Then we can set up another time if my notes warrant it. Or if you decide that I've given you enough information to start, I can make some contacts. I have a good reputation and not above exploiting it." Maddy was making more notes as she spoke.

"Why don't we just set up tomorrow night and meet then? I'm sure we will all have questions, I know I probably will." Colin said again.

"No, I have another job. I can't miss too much work. As it is I've only just started working there full time and I don't want to screw it up for me. I need the money." She stood to go, gathering her things she didn't notice the look shared between the four men.

"No, you're working enough now. Just working for us and Schaller firm should take up enough of your time as it is. If you need money, I'll give it to you. In fact, I'll pay your rent as well; tell me who to see about setting it up." Kyle was poised to take notes and do just what he'd proposed. Aaron thought about helping him but decided the only way some people were to learn was to have it beaten into their heads.

"Fuck Kyle, do you have a fucking death warrant?" Though Bradley had said it low, Maddy still heard him.

"Yeah Kyle, do you?" She advanced on him, like a steam roller Aaron thought, a beautiful mad steamroller. "What makes you think you have any rights whatsoever to tell me what I can and cannot do? And pay my rent, my rent? I'll have you know that I've been taking care of my own bills for quite some time now, and I don't need some big man to take care of me. Why all the nerve, I should...I should...grrr, I should just kick your nuts up to around your eyeballs and be done with it." She had him backed against the wall and was poking her finger in his chest with each word.

Aaron glanced around the room and noticed that they all but him had abandoned ship, leaving poor Kyle to sink or swim on his own.

When Kyle lifted his hand and gently caressed his finger down her cheek, Aaron wanted to applaud for him. Aaron heard her breath caught. Kyle slowly slid his hand and cupped the back of her head and drew her to him, to his body and his mouth. Aaron was just standing to leave when he heard Kyle say something he was sure was going to get him staked yet.

"Madison, I've dreamed of this, of tasting you. I want you, I want you so bad. This is what gives me the right, love; this is why I'll do this."

He watched Kyle stiffen. Then the man simply fell to the floor, holding his nuts like they were a lifeline. Aaron didn't move, he wasn't stupid. A pissed off woman sometimes didn't care who was in her way when she wanted to leave and he didn't want to 'poke the bear' as he'd heard said before.

When she stormed past him without a word, he remained there until he heard the front door close with a bang. Walking over to Kyle he looked down at the man.

"Will you ever learn? I'm beginning to think you won't." Aaron leaned over and picked his friend up. "Come on old boy. Let me get you to bed before sunrise fires you."

"Aaron," Kyle groaned. "I fucking hate you."

Aaron laughed all the way to the sub levels where he dropped Kyle on his bed and laughed all the way to his own room that he shared with his lovely Sara. Yes, Aaron thought, this was going to be a great deal of fun.

Chapter Thirteen

"You will not make demandsss tonight, my love. You are mine to rule, yesss to rule. Come to me, let me ssseee you, tasste you. Tell me yesss." It sounded more confident today, but no less demanding.

They were in the room again, the void. The air, or lack of it burned her, seared her throat and lungs with every breath. The pulled muscle in her back ached with renewed pain, it too burning her.

"Who are you? Please, tell me who you are?" She knew this was a dream. It had to be a dream.

"I'm no dreamsss, I am real. Patcalusss, me, I'm Patcalusss, for you. You are mine. You were promisssed to me. I demand you come to me. Me. You must say it, that you will come to me."

She suddenly knew it could read her feelings, was somehow feeding from them. She wasn't sure how she knew. There was something else, something she was supposed to do, or say...what was it?

"No," he shouted through her mind. *"Me, you mussst listen to me. You were promised to me, I will have you. Breed, you will breed for me, only for Patcalussss."*

"You aren't real, you aren't real. Get out of my head. I will breed for no one, never." Her head hurt, her body felt hot and heavy and the incredible pain.

Like before the scream tore from her and into her. Whatever it was it was pissed. She arched up out of her bed and onto the floor, screaming over and over. She had finally collapsed by the time they had broken down the door.

No one called the police, or an ambulance. In this building both or either could get you killed. One of the guys simply picked Maddy up and put her back into her bed and Marcie wiped down her face until she felt soggy, her pillow soaked.

"You okay sweetmeats? Gotta tell ya, you got a great set of lungs on you there. I'm thinking maybe you outter go out to singing or something with those puppies. Girl, yeah you know it." Marcie meant well, at least Maddy hoped she did. One could never tell.

"Yes, I'm better. Just another bad dream. I'll be okay now. Thanks." She started to sit up and pain grabbed her by the throat and stopped her lungs moving. Frozen in place with it, she tried to remember, to think even what the hell she had done.

"Wow, oh wow, you're like white, like sheet white. Well not all sheets, mine you know are red, 'Oh Baby Red' I think they should be called. Then Frank's his 'er black. Some silky shit or something. When you get going though, we damn near fuck ourselves right outta bed. You getting up now?"

Maddy had to get away from her, her head was splitting and she was thirsty. So thirsty. She stumbled to her dresser where she always had bottled water and nearly tore the lid from the bottle in her haste to get it opened. She drank it down in one draw. She reached for the second bottle and with a little more fineness, opened it and drained it as well. The water hit her empty stomach hard, making her gag and cough. Dropping to her knees she threw up all the water and bile into the trash can.

"Fuck me girl, that ain't right. You wanna maybe have me, I don't know, call somebody for ya. Cause, you know, fuck that ain't right." Marcie moved toward the broken door. Maddy didn't care. She just wanted to die, to crawl into a tight ball and die.

It was an hour later before she could sit up and another thirty minutes before she stood. Thankfully she only needed to use her laptop for the next couple of hours then she'd be able to take a shower and go to work. Hopefully. 'Fuck girl, that ain't right, well no shit!' she thought.

By the time she finished working on the proposal for the men and decided that they needed a business name she decided she was feeling a little better. After the hot shower, she was nearly human feeling again.

"I need to ask Mr. Wolff if he feels human, just for comparison purposes," she said with a giggle.

Maddy had only been to sleep for an hour before the dream hit, so by the time she'd made it to the MacManus estate it was only one thirty. By then everyone but Sally and Duncan were gone or to bed or coffin, whatever she thought.

"These are for the men. They're labeled for them. I left a phone number where I'll be tonight if anyone has any questions." Maddy could smell the muffins in the oven and wanted one in the worse way. Instead she asked for a glass of water, no ice please.

"If you do not mind my saying Miss, you do not look so well. Are you unwell?" Duncan asked, concern coloring his voice. She smiled at him. She knew she looked like shit, she'd seen what she'd looked like when she'd left home. Dark circles under her eyes, pain riddled her body. Kyle, she grinned would have no trouble telling her what she looked like.

"Yeah, I'm okay. I had a bad dream that's all. Just a bad dream. Duncan, I'm really sorry about this, but do you think I can have one of those muffins? They smell heavenly."

Her mouth was watering now, she didn't know what she would have done if he'd of said no. But he didn't, he sat her down and found her a plate and Miss Penny fixed her a glass of iced tea. Before too long she was wolfing down her third muffin and enjoying a second glass of the best tasting tea she'd ever drank.

"I feel like such a pig. I hope that those weren't for anything special. You have to let me pay you for them. I've never…I was suddenly so hungry. I guess it was from throwing up, but I feel so much better. How much do I owe you?" She had been dragging out her wallet, and thinking she didn't have much, but she would certainly give him all she had and more for what he'd done for her.

"Nonsense. I have baked them for the household and you are a part of it now. You will just take the rest with you. I have already wrapped them up. Miss Penny, see if you can find her a nice jug please? Good girl," he told the older woman when she handed him one. "and some of her lovely tea to go with them as well." Despite her best efforts, she left with seven more muffins and a thermos of iced tea.

Maddy was at work by four-thirty and had her fruit cut and the glasses gleaming by the time the bar opened at five. The girls had shown up while she was finishing up.

"You know girl, you look a little under the weather, you feeling fine," Nips asked as she sat on one of the bar stools.

Maddy explained about having a bad dream to Pink Nips, hopefully her stage name and not something her parents had actually picked out for her, and after she'd been starting at Maddy for about ten minutes, she finally told her how to sleep better.

"Ah girl, you gotta get laid and good and laid, not one of them quickies. One that lasts the night and you walk funny the next day kinda laid."

"She's gotta meet a man first, don't ya, Mad?" Marabeth was the oldest stripper working at Puss n' Boots at forty-four. She must still *'have it'* as they were good at saying, because she brought in about two grand a week in tips alone.

"I've met one, thanks. And I didn't care for him. He's an arrogant prick and I'd rather sleep alone than be bossed around, thanks. Besides, he didn't want me when he had me." Maddy still stung a little about Kyle being sorry that he'd kissed her, but there wasn't a whole lot she could do about it.

"Show time ladies and Marabeth. And leave Mad Hatter alone. Men suck." Paul said with mock anger, as he winked at Maddy and went to the kitchen to get the grill started up.

The bar served a few dinner items from six until eleven or so and Paul did all the cooking. Jake, his son did the short order stuff and kept the pots and pans up. It worked out well for them as a family, the family that bar keeps together drinks together, and all that.

~~~

"Puss n' Boots, what do you want?" Aaron pulled the phone from his ear and stared at it. Okay, he thought, that couldn't have been right.

"I'm sorry, what did you say?" The surly voice on the other end confirmed that he had indeed heard them correctly. "Ah, well then is Madison Harm there by any chance?"

"Yeah, she's standing on the bar," the man on the phone told him. "She's about to pistol whip some asshole who got fresh with Shelly. Hang a minute."

The phone was set down on the bar with a bang. Aaron listened to the noises in the back ground and could hear Maddy telling some '*small minded, tiny dicked, poophead to either leave on his own, or she'd help him out via the meat wagon*' or something along those lines. She worked in a bar and by the sounds of it an unsafe bar.

"What," she snapped.

"This is Aaron MacManus. What the hell is going on over there? I'm assuming this is 'Puss n' Boots', it's a bar?"

"Some nights," she told him with a great deal of anger. "I have to tell a customer that just because he's twenty-one it doesn't give him the rights to grab someone's tits as he called them. And since he hit the bartender—me in this case I had to show him who's boss."

"And what was his answer to that may I ask." Aaron could feel his anger about to boil over. This woman, he decided had a death wish.

"Before or after he spit on me? I pistolwhipped him. You don't screw around with the bartender here. Who would make the fucking drinks?"

"Is it safe for you to be working in a place that you have to pistolwhip someone into submission?" He knew his voice was calm, but that wasn't what he was feeling. Aaron had had fifteen minutes of listening to the byplay between her and the young punk and his anger had gown with each passing minutes. Someone needed to take her into hand.

"It was that or kill him, and I can't be your lawyer if I go to jail for murder," her voice sounded so reasonable that he wanted to murder her. "Besides, I don't see where this is any of your business Mr. MacManus. I will do the job you want me to do and if you have a problem with that job, then you can ask me to stop, otherwise, fuck off. My jaw hurts and right now I'm not in the mood to be reprimanded by my daddy."

"Let's just say I'm making it my business. I want you to quit that job and I—fuck." She'd hung up on him, just put the phone in the cradle and ended the call. He dialed the number again.

"Puss n' Boots. What can I do to you?" This voice was chipper, almost childlike most assuredly not Madison.

"Madison Harm. Tell her it's Aaron MacManus."

Aaron was pissed off. He realized that barking at the woman who answered the phone wasn't fair, but no one hung up on him, damn it.

"Yes, Mr. MacManus. What may I assist you with this evening?" Her voice was sweet and congenial, polite even. That for some reason made him madder.

"You will not hang—son of a bitch!"

She'd done it again. Damn her. He started to throw the phone across the room but Kyle walked in instead. Okay, he thought play fire with fire.

"Do you have any idea where your mate is right this moment?"

Chapter Fourteen

"Oh baby, you should see what just walked in. Not one, not two, not even three, but four of the most drop dead, well hung, tight assed men I have ever seen. And you know what else…" Shelly paused for effect. And before someone got up to hit her, she said, "They're asking for the Mad Hatter."

"Well fuck, he brought the whole fucking gang down, didn't he."

Maddy figured he'd do something. But thought he'd just yell at her tomorrow, and maybe, just maybe tell Kyle, not that she'd given much thought to what he might think, but still…

All the girls went to stand behind the bar to watch the men walk toward the bar. Maddy stayed where she was, and finished her burger. She didn't get a meal with meat often, so she was going to enjoy it. When she walked out they each had a draft in front of them and a bowl of the bars only claim to fame, pepper corn.

It was popcorn with so much pepper on it that it was black and so hot that anyone who ate even one handful needed several drinks to quince their throat. Maddy thought that it tasted nasty and marveled that anyone would even think about putting any in their mouth.

"Beers? Popcorn? What are you trying to do, blend. I got news for you, it's not working. Men like you do not frequent bars like Puss n' Boots. What do you want? I'm working." She walked to the other end of the bar when they didn't answer and pulled two drafts and made two other drinks.

"I want to talk to you. Right now." She didn't even see Kyle move. One minute he was sitting with the other three men then he was dragging her through the bar like she was an errant child and he was going to punish her. They were almost to the door when Paul was in front of them.

"Let her go. You let her go, or I use this bat on your head. You have a choice. Well, not really 'cause that one was the only one I was giving you. Nobody drags the Hatter around. Paul stood there with one of his wooden bats in his hand pounding it into the other one." Paul didn't get involved in any violence, but paid people to do it for him. Maddy was both pleased and afraid for him.

"This isn't any of your concern. Madison and I need to have a few words." Kyle pushed her behind him. When she tried to step around him, he pushed her back.

"When you walked into my bar and grabbed my bartender, you made it my business. Now, I ain't gonna tell you again, let her go." Paul began to pound the bat in his hand harder.

"Madison, you need to tell this man that its fine." He turned his back to the man and looked at her, and opened his mouth. His fangs were dropped and his eyes were a deep red. "I don't want to hurt him, and you know that I can. Tell him to go back inside and no one will get hurt."

Without looking away from Kyle she assured Paul that everything was fine, she'd only be a few minutes. Turning on her heel and not even waiting for him to follow, she walked out into the night.

"What the fuck was that all about? What, were you gonna bite him, maybe drain him? And for what? To prove a point? If so, then you need to explain to me what the point might have been, because you just threatened my friend. And he was—"

He jerked her to him and kissed her. The kiss was quick. And when he moved his mouth down along her throat, her knees began to tremble. When he pulled away to explain to her what he'd been doing, she started snapping again.

"No, I won't have you…" She couldn't think, his mouth was doing wonderful things to hers and her body liked it. "Please, don't Kyle, I can't…" Breathing became difficult, and her body had suddenly had a mind of its own. She kept telling it no, no and it was saying fuck off, yes, yes.

~~~

Cupping her ass in his hands, he pressed her core, her heat to his cock. He groaned against her mouth need slammed into him. He took the two steps to the building, held her against the wall and devoured her, his tongue taking and tasting, dancing the lover's dance of wet heat of her mouth. Moving his hands down to her thighs he pulled her up that that her legs wrapped around his hips then lower so he could moved hard back and forth against her. Her scent, her arousal poured over him.

"Madison, I want you baby."

With his hands free now he moved up her waist, then further and cupped the luscious breast in his hand. Thumbing the hard nipple, feeling the erect little nub through her bra and tee shirt he moaned against her mouth. His cock was straining against the fabric of his pants and aching to be inside of her. Reaching between them he pressed his thumb against her clit hard, again and again. Her whimpers of need were driving him closer and closer to the edge. He pulled her away from him and nearly lost it when she cried out.

Now! He needed her now. Kyle pulled open the button on her pants and felt her tugging at the buckle of his pants at the same time, getting the little zipper down proved to be nearly impossible for him to comprehend and was close to ripping it off when the back door opened and a man stepped out onto the back lot. Both of them froze. He moved her to keep the other man from seeing her, and then pulled the shadows around them both.

Breathing hard and holding her close, he closed his eyes. Fuck, he thought, he wasn't some ranty kid on his first night out; he was a fourteen hundred year old vampire. Who nearly took his mate for the first time against the wall of a strip joint.

"Madison, I want you to come with me, come home with me please?" He was begging and frankly didn't give a shit who knew. This woman had brought him to his knees every time he was near her he came a little closer to going over the edge. Not that it didn't sound appealing but he needed to focus.

"I can't, I... Shit, I have to work, I...no we can't. I have to go inside. Move. Move out of my way."

Kyle leaned hard against the wall when she went inside. He was out of his league. He was out of his mind but he knew one thing. He wanted her with every cell in his body.

Aaron was sitting at one of the bars few tables, when Kyle walked back in. He was watching Maddy work behind the bar as she began making a draft. There was no one there to drink it, and the girls were avoiding her too. Kyle watched as Aaron stood up and walked over to her and took a stool.

"You look well and truly kissed Madison Harm." When she glared at him, he threw back his head and laughed. Kyle could hear their conversation and wasn't all that thrilled about Aaron with his mate.

"You know I really hate you." There was a catch in her voice and her lips were swollen from their kisses. It was everything he could do not to go and get her and finish what they'd started.

"No you don't," Aaron told her softly. "You know I had to do it. I had to make him aware of how unsafe it is for you here. He can't survive without you, you are his life blood."

"I don't understand. How can I be his life blood, I'm not a…vampire." She whispered the word as if she was afraid someone would overhear them. Kyle smiled to himself. She would be a fantastic mate.

"No, you're not one, yet. But you are his mate." He turned to watch him as he sat with Colin and Bradley. Kyle saluted him and Aaron grinned back at him. Aaron turned to look at Maddy.

"No, you're mistaken. I'm not, I'm not anyone's anything. I don't even know what that means, but I'm sure it's not me. He…he doesn't want me. He…I…we have, I mean we started, then he pushed me…he told me he was sorry, sorry that he touched me. You're mistaken, he doesn't want me. Now, I have to work, I need this job." She walked away from him and began filling orders for the waitresses.

~~~

For nearly three hours she worked without stopping, never looking up from her drinks other than to see who she was working with. When Shelly reminded her it was two-thirty and last call Maddy rang the big bell and began cleaning glasses and breaking down the bar. By four o'clock she had cleaned the last of the tables and had helped the waitresses stack the chairs onto the tables. By five she was walking out the door with Jake and Shelly close behind. It wasn't until Jake grabbed her arm that she became aware of the man next to her car. It was Kyle.

"I'll see her home."Jake stood there and waited for Maddy to tell him what to do. He was barely twenty years old, only four years her junior, but sometimes she felt old enough to be his mother.

"It's okay Jake, thanks" She watched them walk away and waved as they got into Shelly's old car and drove home. Paul had left to go to the police station and file a complaint against the kid from earlier. She turned back to Kyle and stared at him until he shifted uncomfortably against the car. "Why are you here?"

Standing, he leaned over her, his breath fanning against her cheek, his body heat radiating out to her.

"Because I'm going to take you home, then I'm going to take you to bed and fuck you for the rest of the night."

When he held his hand out for her keys, she handed to him without a fight. He opened the passenger side door for her and waited until she was seated and buckled before he leaned into the car and kissed her with a quick brush of his lips against hers.

Once he was settled on under the steering wheel, squashed up, but able to drive, he turned to her for an address. She gave it to him and off they went. Neither said a word the entire way. Each lost in their own thoughts. When he pulled in front of the building she shared with eighteen other people he simply pulled away and drove in the opposite direction.

"I think you might have missed the fact that I lived back there." She wasn't amused. She was tired and she wanted to get some sleep. She had things to do tomorrow.

"I think you might have missed the fact that that place is a hell hole and a dive. We're going to my place." He drove up to the gate of the MacManus mansion and pushed in a code and had the doors swinging open before anyone was waked up by the alarm.

"This is Mr. MacManus' house. You live here."

Things were starting to fall into place, why he was always here, and the fact that he and Aaron were on such good terms, even the talk in the bar tonight.

"He told you didn't he? He told you what I said and you came back there to prove something to him. This is some macho trip, to prove what, that you can make me hurt. I want you to take me back home. I'm…give me my keys, I'm going home."

"No." He got out of the car and went around to her side and pulled on the door handle. When she wouldn't unlock it, he used the key, unlocked it and opened her door. Instead of seeing if she'd get out on her own, he reached in and ripped the seatbelt from the mechanism and yanked her out and threw her over his shoulder.

"Put me down you shit head. I mean it, and you're paying for that seatbelt. I don't know who you think you are throwing me around like a…a sack of potatoes but I've…ouch, you bastard!"

He swatted her ass again. "Shut up, you'll wake the house up. The kids have school tomorrow."

"And thankfully they sleep like the dead. Hello, Maddy." Maddy lifted her head to see Sara sitting in the kitchen. "I see you've been shanghaied into coming back. Kyle, do be nice."

"Mrs. MacManus. Hummm, he was just taking me home." She tried to look at dignified as she could while hanging upside down from his shoulder, not to mention his butt was all she could see.

"No I'm not taking you anywhere but to my bed. Now hush up. Night Sara." He kissed her cheek and hoisted Maddy higher onto his shoulder and left the kitchen. Maddy used the time to think of ways to murder him in his sleep. Sara's laughter following them.

He tossed her onto his bed and she was up before she took a second bounce. Kyle just pushed her back again. He started taking off his shirt, slowly unbuttoning the buttons. When she stood again, he pushed her back.

"Fuck! Stop that. You…you poop head. She…she thinks were going to, to…you know." She didn't move, but laid there and watched him.

"No she doesn't think, Maddy. She knows what we're going to do. And we are. A lot." He tossed the shirt onto the chair and began unbuckling his belt and toeing off his shoes.

Maddy watched him as each button separated from the tiny hole, as it reveled its treasure beneath. When he pulled his belt from the loops and threw it across the room her eyes tracked it, and then came back to him and his pants. He stopped when he unsnapped them.

"Give me your foot." Still on her back, she put her foot into his hand and watched as he unlaced her boot slowly and removed it from her foot. Without asking she handed him her other foot and watched as he gave it the same treatment.

She could feel her heart pounding, and she felt breathless. Everytime his finger brushed against her skin, held her ankle in his palms she felt her body expand, tightened.

He reached for her hand and helped her stand up. Barely touching her, afraid to really, he began unbraiding her hair. When he was finished, he looked into her eyes.

"I want you. I've never wanted a woman like I do you Madison. If you don't want to do this, tell me and I'll take you home right now. No, that's not true. I'll take you upstairs to one of the bedrooms on the upper floors. I can't take you back to that house. You have to know that it isn't safe."

"Yes, I know. I don't want to go anywhere." Her voice was low and gravely, need for him and what the need for her promised in his own eyes making her achy.

"I…we bite. During sex, we bite our partners. If that makes you squeamish or scared, I won't. I'll be careful and not bite you. I won't lie to you Madison, the thought of sinking my fangs into your vein and drinking from you while I'm inside of you is the most erotic thing I've ever imaged." He was panting. She knew just how he felt. She wanted him to rip the clothes from her and take was nearly crippling her. And his scent was making her nearly wild with his need to taste her.

Maddy looked at him and was overwhelmed with need. Need to touch, taste, and to feel. She reached down to the hem of her tee shirt and pulled it up and over her head, tossing it over to where he had thrown his own shirt. She reached up to the front clasp of her bra and unhooked it, but he stayed her hands when she made to remove it too. Reverently he traced her skin along the top of it and to the opening. Without taking his eyes from hers, he pulled the ends apart to free her from the material. He kissed her, a small brush of his lips against her once, twice then pulled her to him, crushing her breasts to him. As he swept his tongue into her mouth, he palmed her breasts, both of them in his hands and sank them onto the bed.

"Mine."

Chapter Fifteen

Kyle rolled to his side and looked down at the woman beside him. He marveled again at her body, now his. He ran his hand down her waist and just to the top of her pants where the zipper was still halfway up. Slowly, back and forth he touched her. Then pinching the small tab between his fingers he leaned down and ran his hot tongue over the stiffened peak of her nipple. When she bowed up, pressing more of her full breast into his mouth, he suckled at her hard, pulling her deeper in. Once the zipper was pulled completely down, he dipped his finger into her pants, past her panties and into her creamy heat. Her moan was like a hot knife being driven into him, his cock strained to be free and into her.

He sat up now, and stood at the side of the bed, just between her legs which were hanging off the bed at her thighs. He reached down and pulled her pants down her legs and off, dropping them behind him with their other clothes. Her panties were the only thing she had on. He knew that he wouldn't last much longer if they were completely bare so leaving his pants on, he sank down to his knees before her.

Maddy leaned up on her elbows to watch him. His eyes were deep, deep red the red tinge looking at her made him realize that he was close to his beast. The part of him that wanted to take without permission to take what he needed what he wanted.

"I want to taste you. No, I need to taste you. Please, baby."

His hands on her waist, he slowly moved them down to her panties and to the small scrap of silky material between her thighs. He moved enough away to touch the curls beneath and to slid his finger up the seam of her nether lips, gathering her wetness as he did. When he exposed her clit, he leaned in and ran his tongue along the same path and teased the tiny nub. Her legs stiffened and tightened around his head, her fingers tangled in his hair, pulling him tighter and deeper to her.

"Kyle, please, I'm begging you, please, help me please, please, please."

"Madison, Christ, I…Fuck." He stood up and tore the zipper completely out of his pants and jerked them from him, his cock leaped toward her. He fisted himself, jerking his hand up and down, harder, faster. "I don't think…that's an understatement, I don't want to hurt you love, but I need to be inside of you, I can't wait, now, I need you now."

She reached out and wrapped her hand around him, it was hot and he felt his entire body react to her touch. Before he could protest or even whimper at what she was doing to him, she ran her tongue up his shaft and then wrapped her lips around his blood filled crown.

His release hit him hard and he roared with it, her wet heat, her tongue was too much. He grabbed the back of her head and held her tight as he pumped into her, fucking her mouth hard. He couldn't stop; he came and came, his cock and his cum hitting the back of her throat, gagging her.

His cock still hard, still straining for the ultimate release, he lifted her by her waist. Instinctively she settled her legs around him, pulling her up then down onto his cock, he slammed into her. Maddy screamed from the pain, the intrusion, but he didn't stop, couldn't. Over and over he pumped her, slamming her hard against him, onto him. When her legs tightened around him, he fell onto the bed with her beneath him. He never stopped, moving inside of her faster and faster he went.

"Now Kyle, please, bite me now, yes now. I...I, oh god yes." Maddy's climax hit her and with another scream she brought Kyle with her. While his seed poured into her body, his body convulsed inside of her, Kyle tilted her head, exposed her throat and bit her deep in her vein, bringing them both to peak again.

Drinking from her, tasting the spicy hot blood that was her filled him. He knew that for the rest of his days she would sustain him, fill him. When he'd taked all he dared he sealed the tiny prick marks with his tongue and then kissed the tiny wound with a lingering kiss.

Breathing hard, he rolled over onto his back, bringing her with him and tucked her tightly in next to him. His body was covered in sweat and her, and he'd never been happier. He heard her breathing and felt her shutters still racking her slight body. He must have hurt her, he'd been a mad man, uncaring if he'd hurt her or not. Well, that wasn't true, he did care, but Christ when she'd taken him into her hot mouth, he'd thought he'd explode. He gently ran his hand down her spine, pulling her up his body; he leaned to his side to see her face. Her eyes were closed and relaxed. Tiling her chin up he heard her snore, just a tiny little puff of air, but certainly a snore.

Her car was a mess, old and in need of replacing. And there was no way she could live in that building. Not only was it in the worse part of town, but even in the short time he'd been there knew that it was the place to go to get any drugs you wanted. The job was the next thing that had to go, she couldn't work for a bar, a strip bar any longer. The fact that she carried a gun and had a need to scared him too much to think about. No, she and him would need to sit down and map out a plan and very soon. He'd have to ask Aaron tomorrow if he could stay in this realm, and then go about finding a suitable home for the two of them.

He fell asleep with a smile on his face.

Chapter Sixteen

Maddy woke not ten minutes after Kyle had mapped out their entire future and then fallen asleep. She wouldn't have been happy, but in this case, ignorance is bliss. At least for the time being.

She carefully moved out from under his heavy arm and slipped out of the bed. The room was black as pitch, as they were in some sort of sub levels of the basement and there were no windows. Moving quietly, she gathered up her clothes she could find and went to the bathroom and cleaned up. Pulling her hair back into a haphazard ponytail, she went to the door and after opening it, she left to wander around the halls. It hadn't been her plan to do that, but she didn't know the area down here, and had made several wrong turns before finding a staircase up to the main floor.

She decided she wasn't going to think about what had happened, what they had done, what she had done until she got home. But she knew that the sooner she got out the better she'd feel. Stopping in the kitchen, she made herself a cup of hot tea, using a cup from the strainer and the tea from the ceramic container on the counter. The microwave 'ding' nearly made her scream, and when Duncan walked in just as she was sitting down for a minute, she did make a small yelping noise.

111

"Oh, Miss. I did not...you are here. I was not expecting any...I'm sorry, may I fix you something to eat, I'm sure you must be very hungry." He didn't wait on an answer, but began pulling things from the refrigerator and assembling the makings for what appeared to be an omelet.

She was glad his back was to her, because her face had flamed when he assumed she'd be very hungry, which probably meant that he knew she had spent the night in Kyle's bed. Shit, shit, shit.

"Should probably take out an ad in the local rag," she mumbled to herself. She should have known that he'd hear her.

"Did you say something Miss? The children will be down soon. They have school you know. Her Ladyship will transport them in to the school and the rest of the morning will be hers if you would need to speak to her."

"Mr. Duncan, are you trying very nicely to tell me that Mrs. MacManus could answer any questions I might have about the fact that I've just had sex with a vampire and what happens now that he's bit me? That's very sweet of you, but I really need to go home. I have to shower and I've got lots of things to do for the gentlemen today." She was just rinsing her cup out when a whirl wind that resembled two small kids flew into the room, with a very sedate mother behind them.

"Maddy," shouted the children in unison. "You're still here. You should see what we're doing in school today." For the next twenty minutes while they ate their breakfast and talked about what they had been doing in school, organized devastation reigned.

"I've been wanting to talk to you. I got's your message from you Grammie still. Want I should give it to you now?" Maddy had completely forgotten about that. Mac had told her the night they had told her about what they were.

112

"I guess. But I don't know how you know her."

"She came to me. She told me that you have to remember what she told you. You have to fight and to…hummm…I don't remember the last thing. But I know she'll be coming back. She's been here, like every day since you come over. I have to tell her I ain't seen you and she gets all sad. I'll ask her the next time, will you be coming back home tonight?"

Maddy looked up to see Sara looking at her with a raised brow. Maddy hadn't planned on coming back anytime soon, and couldn't think why they'd want her to, or for that matter why they'd think she would. She and Kyle had only had sex, it was great sex, but it was just sex, that didn't make them married or anything.

"Hummm, no Mac, I'm not coming back tonight. I have to work." She didn't miss the look that past between Sara and Duncan, but decided it didn't matter, she had to work.

"What's this, my favorite children are going off to school without a hug to their papa?? Oh what ever shall I do?" Aaron's timing was just a little too soon to suit Maddy, and tried to make a hasty exit before he started asking question as well. Or worse yet, Kyle decided to make an appearance.

"Thank you for breakfast Mr. Duncan, Mr. and Mrs. MacManus, you have a lovely day. I'm outta here." She moved to the door and grabbed her jacket and shoes.

"A word Ms. Harm if you please? We need to have a talk about what happened last night." Maddy's face couldn't have gotten any hotter if he'd of threw a flame at her. "I meant at the bar, your former place of employment. I assume that at some point last night Kyle and you talked about the fact that that job is not safe for you any longer."

"No, we didn't discuss it, because like you, it isn't any of his business. No one dictates to me Mr. MacManus, not him and especially not you."

"Call me Aaron. And in this matter I insist that—"

"No, I won't call you Aaron. You can insist all you want, but I'm helping you with a project, and nothing more. I don't expect to be invited to barbeques, nor should you expect a Christmas card from me. What has happened between Kyle and I is just that, between Kyle and I. Now, I have to go get tires on my car and I have a job, and some things to do for you guys. I'll let you know by phone what happens with the appointments."

"You work for us, and as my employee you will—"

"I do not work for you. I offered you my help and I'll follow through on my promise to help you with the buildings. But I don't work for you. Now, I'm leaving. Mac, Lizzy you have fun at school."

She opened the door and walked out to her car. She was shaking, from anger or nerves, she wasn't sure. She was half afraid he'd drain her or something. She'd never fought with a vampire before and didn't know if they fought fair or not. When she got to the end of the drive, she pulled over to the side of the road and threw up all that nice breakfast Duncan had prepared just for her. Working for the dangerous bar was looking safer and safer to her all the time. She made her way over to see Danny, her favorite normal person.

"How much do I owe you?" With last night's tip and the money from the whole week she had almost five hundred in cash. Along with the tires, she got her oil changed and the funky noise looked at too. It was a lot of money, but she needed something reliable and it looked like this was it.

"Maddy I'll make you a deal, you represent me in my case Tuesday morning with that broad that says I made a pass at her and I'll overhaul the engine for you. You just pay for parts and the tires." Danny was the only person she knew who could work miracles on her car. Her Grammie had trusted him too. And she knew that he hadn't made any kind of advance on the woman, Danny was gay and had been with the same partner for nearly thirty years.

"What if I lose? It doesn't sound like you're getting a very good deal here." She wasn't worried about losing. She just didn't want him to depend on her too much. Actually, she wasn't sure she wanted anyone to depend on her so much.

"Nah, I'm not worried. Deal?" She shook his hand on the deal and made arrangements to leave her car with him. He even threw in the use of his old clunker truck for her to get around in for the next several days.

Her next stop was the apartment building. The landlord would only replace the door if she caught up with her rent, being two months behind sort of made him testy. "Go figure." She was standing outside her room when Frank showed up.

"Mad Hatter." Maddy had always liked his talkative manner. She grinned at that, he had barely spoke ten words to her since she moved in four years ago.

"Frank. What can I do for you?" Since he wasn't with Marcie she assumed it was he who wanted something and not just tagging along with her.

"Here," he said as he tossed something at her. The large envelope hit her in the chest about two seconds before he ambled away from her and down the hall. Cautiously she opened it.

"Frank! Frank, come back here. What is this?"

It was full of pictures. Naked pictures. Naked pictures of the landlord, and holy Moses he was…he was in bed with Frank. She quickly stuffed them back in the envelope and put them in her backpack. Her mind was spinning, and her stomach was jumping. *Why on earth would he give these to me*, she thought.

Bob Turner, slum lord extraordinary came around the corner just as Frank disappeared into the next apartment. He had the police with him. Shit, shit, shit!

"Ah, Ms Harm, you can be on time for this, but not your rent I see. I'm so glad to see that the young people of today have their priorities straight," Bob snarled at her as he came toward her. "Officers, I want this woman arrested for nonpayment of rent, destruction of property and being a pain in my ass."

"You can't have someone arrested for being a pain in the ass, if that were the case, you'd of been in jail some time ago. Ms Harm, my name is Captain Wolff. Is this man correct? Are you behind in your rent?"

"Wolff. As in Alpha wolf?" She looked him in the eye and waited for his answer. Instead, like his relative, he did something else. He dropped a little of himself and let her see his eyes change. Just for a second, but it was enough.

'Mother fuck. I am so going to get me some garlic and silver shit tonight.' Her voice was low, but she was beginning to realize that all of them seemed to be able to hear a friggin pin drop when they wanted to.

David threw back his head and laughed, startling the man with him and Bob, who took several steps back from him.

"I have some…I may have something that will clear this up. If I could please have a moment with Mr. Turncoat, err I mean Turner. If you could just step this way, I sure the nice…hummm…policeman has better things to do." He followed her into her room and she handed him several pictures from the envelope and waited.

"Son of a fucking bitch," he shouted loud enough for the building to hear. You fucking cunt, where the fuck did you get these?" His face was red from anger, but nothing else. She would have been mortified if someone had had pictures of her like some of those, but he was just angry that she had them.

"I'm very resourceful." She heard David laugh again. Hearing. She'd have to try and remember that one.

Bob walked back into the hall and out of the building. David shouted at him to stop and to ask him what he wanted done now and he yelled that he could fucking shoot her for all he cared and that he wasn't fixing the fucking door ever.

Bob left the building and David sent the other officer with him to get the car and turned to look at Maddy when they were alone. Maddy had a feeling whatever wolf-boy wanted wasn't going to make her day any better.

"I have a message for you Ms Harm. Bradley is my brother and he said to call him or me if you have any more problems here." He handed her a business card with both their names on it and surprise-surprise, a wolf on the front of it.

"Thanks, but I think I can handle myself." She looked down the hall to make sure they were still alone. "Let me ask you something though. Are all the...you know, others like you guys bossy like this? I mean, everytime I turn around one or all of them are telling me where to live, what to do, where to work. Frankly, I'm sick of it. I told them I would help them out and all I've gotten is headaches for my troubles."

Her head was hurting. She didn't get any sleep last night, she'd thrown up all of her breakfast and she had given blood last night. Massaging her temples she looked at him expectantly.

"Yes, but I guess they figure, as do I that we protect those who work for us, and paying you to do a job makes you a part of that group too." He turned then and was headed for the stairs.

"Well, you can tell your brother and whatever else he is, that I don't want his or any of their help. And as they aren't even paying me they need to back the fuck up or I'll press charges." She walked back into her room and didn't even have the satisfaction of being able to slam a door.

"I can give you a quarter percent over what you owe, including back taxes and mortgage." It was only twelve-thirty in the afternoon and every part of her body hurt.

Mr. Simon was her second appointment of the day. And hopefully just one more before she could go back and take a nap before work. She didn't think she could hurt in any more places without being in the hospital. And her head was throbbing like a jack hammer was being used.

"I can't go any less than ten percent. I know you have all the figures, the amount I owe. You have to know that I have to make something off this fiasco."

He looked anything but calm. Three days ago when she'd made this appointment he all but told her to go to hell. But now he was polite, cordial even. She gathered up her things and slipped on her jacket.

"I'll just wait thanks. In less than three weeks the bank is going to take it and sell it to me for whatever they can get me to agree to. You do know that if they don't make enough on the sale that you'll still be responsible for the differences, don't you? I may even get it cheaper. Have a good day." She shook his hand and then turned to leave.

"One percent." She could hear the desperation in his voice now and almost felt sorry for him. Almost.

"Half, and that's the best I can do. The bank says it worth less than the mortgage and taxes together. I need to make a profit too. It's in your best interest to sell now, Mr. Simon."

"Deal. Damn, remind me never to owe you money. What do we do now?" Relief was evident on his face. She had told him that with her buying him out, he could keep his credit rating and come out ahead, and she was sure that had played a large part in this deal.

"I'll contact you tomorrow morning and we can meet at the bank. They've already agreed to pay off the taxes for you from your account. It'll have to be as soon as the bank opens, say around seven-thirty. You aren't my only appointment in the morning Mr. Simon, so if you have any questions, please have them ready then, all right?"

The deal with 'Butt and Buns' she'd made on her first appointment of the morning, a now debunked gym and pastry shop was being settled at eight in the same bank. She had had no trouble getting him to take what she'd offered and had had more fun at this meeting. Or she would have it she hadn't been so ill.

"I own two more buildings in that area," Simon told her as she started to gather up her now signed forms. "Want to get them for the same deal?"

They worked for another hour, and by the time she left his office she had purchased his three buildings and four others from acquaintances of his, all at the same rate of exchange. She was smiling as she pulled up in front of the Con Building. The building was going on the market in a few months she'd heard and was disappointed it wasn't in the area she needed it to be in.

Her appointment with Con didn't go as well as the others had. Having not being able to strike a deal with Mr. Con that made either of them happy she left him with her business card – well her name on a index card and told him when he needed the money to give her a call. She didn't expect him to call her but she would get the building.

"Mr. Duncan, could you have Mr. MacManus call me at *'Puss n' Boots'* when he gets up? Tell him that I've made deals on eight of the buildings and he'll need to meet the parties at the two different banks in the morning." She had called the house knowing that the large vamp wouldn't be awake yet. Or so she had hoped.

"Miss Harm, I believe his Lordship has arisen. Would you like to speak with him now?" She didn't particularly want to, but this way he wouldn't be just showing up unwelcomed at the bar again she figured.

"Sure. I guess." She waited for a minute, wishing she'd of just left a message.

"Ms. Harm, you wanted to speak with me?" She knew that he was still pissed by his tone when he came on the line. She was much too tired and way too sore to care about either.

She relayed all the information about the buildings and what time and where the appointments were.

"Those eight building are less than ten million. That's considerable less than you first assumed," he said in a tone that was entirely different than the snobby one he'd been using when he'd come to the phone.

"Yeah, well, I'm a cheap bitch," Maddy told him still not sure if she liked him. "Can you make those times or not? A Ms Patterson is going to be the one we're dealing with. She is also in charge of another five of those buildings and is willing to deal with you for them. She can be tricky, just a heads up."

"Yes, I've met Ms Patterson. She's a member of Bradley's pack. I don't think we'll have too much trouble with her. But I am aware of her being tricky."

Maddy was quite for several seconds, thinking. "You know, I'm beginning to think no one is who they seem. Between wolf packs, bloodsuckers and magical queens, my life has gone from a 'Driving Miss Daisy' sort of life to one like 'Nightmare on Elm Street' change. With the nightmares and threats to my life, I'm ready to call it quits."

"What threats on your life? Is Kyle aware of them?" She could hear the tone in his voice and she just didn't have the energy to deal with him too.

"Just some things going on that I'm dealing with. Nothing for you to be concerned with. I'm a lawyer, things like this happen. I gotta go, I want to try and take a nap before I go in tonight." She hung up, not carrying if he was finished or not. She was exhausted, her body ached and she wanted to crawl back into that big bed with Kyle, not that she would admit that to anyone.

She didn't get her nap, not only that, but she didn't get anything to eat either. When she got back to her room, all of her things were gone. The door was now fixed and the whole room had been cleaned, cleaner than when she moved in. Maddy stood in the center of the room for five minutes just looking around. That's how Marie and Frank found her.

"I got your stuff, Girlfriend. Me and Frank, we picked it all up from the street and put it in some trash bags we done had. It's in our room. Most of the picture glass was broked. Stupid bastards coulda maybe been a little easier on it. They comed last night late, we's so glad you weren't here to see it. They just comed in and tossed it right outta the winder. Whatcha gonna do now?" The entire time she was talking she was patting Maddy's arm.

"I don't know. I just don't know." She shouldn't have pissed him off, but done was done her Grammie used to say. "I have to go to work. I...did you know them? No, don't tell me. You shouldn't have involved yourselves. Turner could get to you next. Will you keep my stuff until tomorrow? I'll…" *I'll what*, she thought. Clime

Two hours later at the bar she was no closer to her *'I'll what'* than she had been before. It was easier to think now that she was alone. Doing things by habit, she started pulling out the fruit to cut up for drinks and set things up for tonight at the bar, her mind on autopilot.

"What the fuck do you think you're doing?" The voice came out of nowhere and the knife slipped into her arm. Blood poured from the cut immediately and she knew she was in trouble as it gushed from her wrist.

She turned around, thinking to confront Kyle for scaring her and to give him a piece of her mind, but she was alone in the bar. She could see that she'd locked the door even from where she was.

"Where are you, you stupid bastard? You made me cut myself. Come out!" She grabbed a bar towel and wrapped it around her arm, blood soaked through almost as fast as she wrapped. She was beginning to get dizzy. Dizzy and more than a little scared.

"I'm not there yet. I'm speaking to you telepathically. You can do the same. I thought we agreed you weren't working there anymore…why do I feel you're in pain? What's happened to you?"

"I told you I cut myself. I…I think I need help. I…I'm bleeding fast. Oh shit, I'm bleeding to death." Maddy crumbled to the floor.

Chapter Seventeen

By the time Kyle pulled up in front of the bar, the police and ambulance was already there. David and Bradley were just outside the bar waiting for him. Neither man looked all that thrilled with him. Well, he wasn't happy with himself either.

"Where is she? Is she all right?" He tried to rush the men but they held him back.

"She's lost a lot of blood, but otherwise is fine. She'd cut the artery in her wrist. The other girls didn't show up until ten minutes after we'd gotten here. If you hadn't of called us there's no doubt she'd be dead. How did you know?" David asked him.

As all paranormal mates, they couldn't cause harm with intention to their mates. These men would know that. They would know that he hadn't caused her harm and that whatever he'd done to hurt her had been an accident.

"I startled her I think. I barked at her through our link, she didn't know. Shit, this is my fault, I didn't think." He'd nearly gone mad with worry when the link was cut off. As soon as she'd lost consciousness, he'd lost all contact with her. All he knew was that she'd been hurt and that she was getting weaker.

They were wheeling her out of the bar when he looked up and he rushed to be with her. She was still unconscious, and he could feel her heart beat was slow but steady. He could smell her blood and his body reacted to it, not with hunger, but with a need to heal her. There was also the sharp smell of medicine and the medical team who had been touching her. It was everything he could do not to snarl at them to get away from her and let him have her.

Kyle started to go with her when they took her to the hospital, but the medic told him that as close as she had been to dying, they wanted to the extra room to work, just in case. He agreed and said he'd follow them. David and Bradley rode in the cruiser behind Kyle so he wouldn't have any trouble if he was caught speeding. Kyle had just started the Hummer when Aaron and Sara materialized beside him.

"Is she all right? Duncan said you needed us here. I've never been so scared in my entire life." Sara even looked worried as she hugged him. "Duncan said that you left because Maddy had been hurt but he didn't seem to know how what had happened. He was nearly frantic. I thought I was going to have to put him to sleep then read his mind to understand. We have to call him as soon as we know anything."

"Of course we'll call him. I don't know anything other than she's lost a lot of blood and that she's cut her wrist. It's my fault entirely, I didn't...I yelled at her through our link and she must have startled or something. She told me she'd cut herself, that I'd scared her, but I didn't listen. All I was concerned about was that she had disobeyed me, again. Damn it, I don't deserve her." He had given up the keys to Aaron when he'd asked for them. He didn't think he could have driven anyway.

"I think we've all been a little hard on her. I know that I myself have been making demands on her as well. Bradley called me tonight. Did you know that we aren't paying her? That all this work she's been doing, she's been doing on her own time? This morning when David went to arrest her she—"

"Arrest her!! For what? Christ that girl gets into more trouble than I've ever seen. She needs a fucking keeper." Kyle cut himself off when he heard Sara clear her throat. He was doing it again, being bossy and making demands.

"Does she remind you of anyone Aaron," Sara asked softly from the back seat. "I think you two need to back off of her. She's done just fine on her own for some time now and has only had issues since the three of you walked into her life. She'll be laid up for a few days now, and I for one think she could do with a little rest, from everything."

Sara had been just as independent and just as stubborn as his Maddy when Aaron had pushed his way into her life. Not that she regretted it Kyle thought, but it had been a little overwhelming, and she knew about vampires and werewolves. Kyle couldn't imagine what Maddy was going through at the moment.

They arrived at the hospital just as they were wheeling Maddy down to surgery. Kyle was asked to fill out paperwork for Maddy. He decided to claim her as his wife so that there would be no problems about him getting information he needed about her health. She was his damn it. Sara and Aaron went on up to the second floor surgery floor.

By the time he finished and was getting off the elevator, Maddy had been under for nearly an hour. He'd had to guess at most of the personal stuff, date of birth, mothers name and other things. He made a mental note to get this information from her as soon as possible. The nurse had not been amused until he told her they'd only been married a short while and that he was tremendously worried about his new bride. That had changed her tune right now. It was another hour before they had taken her down to recovery and the surgeon had come out to see them.

"Mr. Dixon, your wife is very lucky," she's said as she shook his hand. "If that officer hadn't of came when he did, then we'd be having an entirely different conversation. She had a six inch laceration to her right wrist that severed her artery. She was bleeding fast I would imagine and had she of not stuck her arm into that bucket of ice she would have bled out even sooner. As is was, the cold slowed down the stem of blood. Smart woman, your wife."

David had told the dispatcher, then Kyle so he'd know the story when asked. David had been driving by the bar on his way home and thought he saw someone walking around inside. That explained how they knew she was there and the broken door they had to break to get in.

"When can I see her? Is she awake?" He had been so relieved that she was going to be fine that his next priority had to be seeing her.

"Oh, she's awake all right. Weak, but that hasn't stopped her from being pissed off at you. Says you're not married and that...well, I'll let her explain what her plans for your anatomy is. And just so you know, I can't fix what she has planned for you." With a promise that she would see them all in the morning, she went down the hall laughing.

"Maybe you two should go first, soften her up some." Kyle wasn't afraid of her, but he wasn't stupid either. He knew that if she could, she would try and hurt him and in return hurt herself worse.

"Coward. I'll go in, Aaron you keep eunuch boy here company." Sara walked down the hall and laughed when she heard Aaron laugh and Kyle explain to him how unfunny he thought it was.

"She's not going to be any more happy with you if you put it off you know." Aaron, being a straight forward kind of man thought just getting things over with no matter how unpleasant was better than worry about it.

"Yeah, I know. What am I gonna do with her? She drives me crazy." Before Aaron could comment on that statement the elevator doors opened and poured out the motliest group of people they'd ever seen.

"I swear if'n he hurt her, I'll cut his balls off and feed them to him, that slimy worthless piece of bat shit."

It seemed that Paul had closed the bar. The police were still milling around anyway and had called his bowling buddy Frank to tell him that Maddy had been hurt. It wasn't long before the entire building where she lived, or had lived had found out. Then as word got out that she'd been taken to the hospital, patrons from the bar decided to show their support to the young woman and brave the hospital to go see one of their own. Marie had been the one making the threat not at Kyle, like he'd thought but the slumlord, Bob Turner. Kyle was still trying to figure out the dynamics of the group and what their relationship to Maddy was.

"He had her stuff tossed right outta the winder, the slimy prick. Frank and me, we gots it all for her. Busted up all her purty pictures they did. Girl ain't got but two pairs of them pants she wears and some nice shirts. Under wares a hanging from the fire escape…Just plain ain't right the way he done her, nope ain't right." Marie had a captive audience in Kyle and was giving him all he wanted, and a lot of what he didn't.

"You say this happened tonight?" If that was true and he had no doubt that it did, it seemed Maddy had had a busy day.

"Yeah, right 'afore she comed to work I'd say. Frank'll know, Frank," she shouted. "What time you thinkin Mad Hatter was by the building??" Kyle had already discovered that the poor Frank was asked a lot of questions but seldom if ever was given a chance to answer any of them. "Oh, yeah, it was right 'afore. I remember her saying she'd had to go to work. Poor little bit."

After making arrangements to have Duncan come by and get her things from Marie and Frank, Kyle slipped down to her room.

"I don't think you should be trying to leave just yet Maddy, you've lost a lot of blood." He could hear the anger and pleading tone in Sara's voice and feel her helplessness too.

He stepped into the room to see Sara trying to get a very weak looking Maddy to lie back down. Sara was trying her best not to hurt her and Kyle could see the strain of pain on Maddy's face.

"Madison, I want you to get your little butt back in that bed before I have David come in here and handcuff you to the bed." He'd tried to make it light hearted and in a joking manner, but her pain and weakness hit him like a wall as soon as he came into the room.

"You," she snarled at him. "I want you to get away from here. I never want to see you again. You scared me. I could have died, you stupid pig." Her voice was getting weaker, the fight going out of her and she was waning. He stepped closer to her, knowing that she wouldn't be able to sit upright much longer. "I don't want to…I'm so tired. You need to leave. I have to get to work."

"Paul closed the bar. You're friends are here to see you too. They want to come in and see you to assure themselves that you weren't murdered by your ex-landlord." She was messing around with her gown instead of listening to him. "Here, let me help you with that."

She'd been struggling and had it all tangled up in the IV. His mouth watered at the sight of her exposed breast that she had inadvertently showed him trying to get herself untangled. Now was not the time he had to keep telling himself. Later, there would be plenty of time for that later. He had just gotten her snapped back together when she collapsed into him.

"I don't feel so good. My head is all fuzzy and I feel like I've been drained dry. Did you do that?" She looked fuzzy too he thought, and cute. He wanted to lean down and kiss her until they were both fuzzy.

"No, I didn't drain you, you cut yourself. Contrary to popular myth, a single vampire cannot drain a human in one sitting. There are two and a half gallons of blood, and the average stomach can only hold about half a gallon of liquid at one time. It would take three or four of us about two days to do that." He'd babbled off facts to keep himself from picking her up and crushing her to him. Or better yet, him taking her home with him to heal her and care for himself. He did pick her up though and put her back into the bed.

"That was way too much information, thank you very much. I'm only going to rest here for a minute," she told him tiredly and laid back down. "I have things to do today, and I don't want to slack off, I worked too hard to…"

Her voice had gotten weaker as she spoke until she just drifted off to sleep. He reached up to her forehead and touched her gently and put her into a much deeper, restful sleep. She could cuss him all she wanted later. In fact he'd love it if she did but right now he was in charge.

~~~

"I've been waiting for you my lovely. Yesss. You've been hiding from me, your true love. I am angry with you. Yesss, angry indeed." The voice was back so was the room, only this time there was an odor, a smell of burnt something.

"Go away. I don't know who you are, but I want you to go away." Maddy had had enough of men making claims and demands on her.

"*I will come for you in two daysss, you will be ready then, your body to receive my seedsss. A child, we will have many, but this one will be my ssson. I will wait no longer. You were promised to me.*" He had said that before, she remembered that now.

"Your nuts, I wasn't promised to anyone. And I won't go with you in two days or two years. You're just shit out of luck hiss boy, now scram." Something to remember, she needed to remember something else.

The pain ripped through her like a thousand knives tearing at her skin and muscle. She felt her shoulder burn like a hot poker had been laid across it, so hot it seared into her skin and felt as if it would burn right through her. She screamed, and screamed, waking everyone in the bed one floor up and the other below her and all the patients on the same floor. The nurses came rushing into the room to see Kyle leaning over her with her hands above her head and his large body across her small petit one.

"Hurry, help me before she hurts herself," she heard him shout. "Someone get that stupid thing off her before I yank it from the wall."

Maddy had no idea what it was but she hoped it was the poker. Before she could ask, before she could gather enough strength to scream again she heard him say sleep and the darkness rushed up to claim her once again.

Maddy woke and looked around the room, trying to decide where she was and how she had gotten there. There were also strange people in the room with her. She tried to make out who they were when one of them spoke.

"We aren't strange really as much as we are strangers. I've always hated that way of saying you don't know someone when in fact you're just saying they're strange. I'm Elizabeth and this is my daughter Savannah. Melody, her daughter and my granddaughter will be along shortly. She had some last minute royal duties to perform and couldn't get away."

"Of course she did. And I only thought you were strange because you were sitting there looking at me like I've got six heads, when in fact I don't." Maddy felt as if she were Alice and had fallen down the rabbit hole.

"Oh that's a good one considering. I so love Alice in Wonderland. I met the author, a Charles Lutwidge Dodgson some years ago, very strange man that one. He changed his name to write you know. How are you feeling otherwise?" The other woman, Savannah had asked, but Maddy felt that she already knew that.

"I would very much like it if you'd stop reading my mind, if that is what you're doing. That jackass Kyle doing that is what got me in here in the first place. Yelling at me, then saying as if it were nothing in the world, 'I'm speaking to you telepathically' like I'm fucking supposed to know that," she flushed when she realized she was ranting at the strangers. But she couldn't seem to stop. "Well it made me jump. Of course I should have been paying better attention, but I had had a pretty shitty day up until then and…who did you say was running behind again?" She'd been on a tangent and the fact that someone had royal duties just registered with her.

"My granddaughter, Melody, she's the Queen of magic. We thought you'd take our news better if the men were gone. She said she's on her way; we just have to make sure you're prepared for her coming in the room. Are you, prepared I mean?" Maddy could only nod. Either she was off her rocker, or these women were. She had a feeling they were as sane as they came.

"Thank you dear." Savannah patted her on the head and covered Maddy's eyes. "It can be a bit disconcerting the first time you see it, so I'll help you out."

When she was able to see again, there stood a beautiful woman dressed in a robe and crown. The robe was long and made to look like the earth, the colors fading from the ground up to the sky. The crown was very bejeweled with rubies, emeralds and diamonds all centered on a very ornate tree with apples and other fruits.

"Is that for my benefit, or do you have to where that all the time?" Maddy knew it was rude, the lady was some sort of queen or something, but she thought maybe if she played along for a while, they'd give her more of the drugs she was obviously taking.

"Yours," she told her with a smile. "Too much?" Maddy nodded. She wasn't sure what else to do. "Yeah, I thought so too. But Sara, she's my cousin said you'd had a hard time of it and didn't really believe in any of this, so I thought, what the hell." And suddenly she was in jeans and a tee shirt. "Ah, much better. I'm Melody, Mistress of Light, Keeper of all Magic, yada, yada. I'm here to keep you company for awhile and to see if you're human."

"Okay, but just so you know I...hummm, I kinda already know what I am. Human. A nutty as a fruitcake human, but human all the same. And I need to get out of here. I have to meet with the bankers at eight in the morning with Mr. MacManus." She started to rise, but was stopped by the handcuff at her unwrapped wrist and her ankle.

"You had a bad dream and they were afraid you'd hurt yourself again. The leather straps they used couldn't hold you so they resorted to those. Beastly things, but you were fighting pretty hard," Savannah said with another pat to her arm. "You should have seen poor Kyle. We thought the man was going to tear that doctor's arm right out of the socket for making you moan. As for the meeting with Aaron, that was three days ago love. You've been in here for four days."

Savannah had seated herself on the side of her bed and was fingering the cuffs. And before Maddy knew it the cuffs were off her but still closed and attached to the bed. "We'll have to put you back in them before we leave, don't want you to have to try and explain how you got out."

"No, no of course not. I...thank you, I think. But I couldn't have been here for four days. He said that he was coming—" Maddy stopped suddenly, not sure she wanted these people to know about that part of the dream. She was supposed to remember something. Her Grammie told her to...something.

"I'm sure she knew what you were and gave you the means to fight your tormentor," Mel said as she sat down. The chair just suddenly appeared behind her. "And you aren't human. Well not totally I think. You are half human but the other part I'm not sure yet. I'd like to touch you please? You have a spell on you, a protection charm. A very strong one if it's kept me from feeling you all these years."

Maddy felt her first tingle of fear. Not of these women but of what they would tell her. She had a feeling that this was not going to end well. Not for her at any rate. She pulled her arm back and tucked it under the sheet.

"I...I'm sure you're mistaken. I'm just a normal person. Not that you aren't normal or a person, it's just that I'm not half anything. Well that's probably not true, right now I feel about half baked." She looked at the three women and felt the room closing in on her. She could feel the air being sucked out as she sat there. "I can't breathe, I...I need some air."

Frantically she pulled at the IV in her arm and tried to get the rails down on the bed at the same time. It wasn't until she felt

Savannah's touch that she calmed down. It was warm and comforting. Her heart rate seemed to slow and her breathing became easier.

"Shhhh, it's all right. You're just a little stressed right now. Close your eyes." Maddy did as Savannah asked. "That's it. Calm breaths Maddy, in and out. Good girl, now I want you to think of Kyle, reach for him mentally, see him in your mind. When you have a clear picture, I want you to say his name, form the word in your head and wake him." Maddy nodded and did as she instructed, not really sure why but said his name.

"Kyle?" She felt a little silly, but was immediately engulfed in a glow of warmth. She felt him, felt him as if he were standing right next to her.

"Madison, are you all right?" She heard the concern in his voice and the slight amusement too.

"I...You're there. I didn't know what to expect, but there you are. Where are you? I mean, I'm sorry, it's none of my business where you are." She felt better for just being able to speak to him, to hear his voice. That scared her a little, but she didn't want to analyze that just now.

"You can talk to me anytime you want. I'll always be here for you." His laughter seemed to move over her and through her. *"I'm at the mansion in my lair. My sheets smell of you. I wouldn't let Duncan change them. I wanted to be able to smell you whenever I wanted. I want to bring you back her and make love to you. Would you like that Love, to come back here and fuck each other senseless?"*

She felt his arousal then, and he sent her graphic thoughts of them together. Maddy felt her body flame up and her pussy expand, her need immediate. She wanted him, right now and she didn't care how.

"I guess you were able to talk to him." Maddy had forgotten that they were there, and blushed harder because she was sure they knew what they had been talking about. "We don't cross the line into mates, but from your blush I'd say it would be worth the risk. Feel better now?" Maddy realized that Savannah had done that to make her feel better and to calm her.

"Thank you. Yes, I feel much better." She felt the connection between her and Kyle lessen and knew that he'd fallen back into a light sleep. "You say that I'm not completely human, how do you know?" Might as well join them she thought, it was much easier than fighting them.

"Good girl. I'll be in to see you when the sun is going down. You and I have much to talk about." And with a finally erotic thought Kyle fell into a deeper sleep. She could still feel him there, but she could also feel him at rest.

"I'm not sure, but something wants to get to you. I can smell it on you now. And Kyle told us he could smell it on you a few days ago." Mel had pulled her chair closer and put a small basket of fruit on the little hospital table that hung across the bed, after taking an apple she handed the whole thing to Maddy.

"That's right, I remember now. He asked me what I'd been burning. It was the next morning. The voice had come to me that night." She pulled an apple out as well and was slightly disconcerted that one appeared in the same place to replace it. She looked up at Mel and was winked at.

"It's my basket. I love fruit and take it with me everywhere. The fact that it replaced the fruit you took tells me that you have some magic in you, strong magic. Otherwise it would have waited until you were no longer present or not looking to do so." *Of course* Maddy thought, a basket that knew more about her than she did.

"So this is a test of sorts." Anger made her mouthy...well more so anyway. "What's next, you sit down a hat and I pull a rabbit out? I don't like being put on display like some kind of performing monkey."

"The basket wasn't a test I assure you. I simply wanted you to eat more fruit. Living with a vampire can be sorta draining, no pun intended. I was more surprised than you were the basket accepted you." Mel wasn't mad or upset Maddy could see. She seemed amused more than anything.

"So, I have magic," Maddy asked as she took a bite of the apple half expecting it to do something to freak her out. "What kind of tests do you have to throw at me?"

"I'd like to take your bandage off if you don't mind. You were cut very badly just a few days ago and I want to see how well you've healed." Elizabeth moved toward the bed as she spoke.

"Okay. But what do you hope this proves?" Maddy began unwrapping the gauze not sure why she was complying and more than a little afraid that she was.

She was very careful not to bump the wound. When she was perhaps two or three layers from the skin she stopped. Her stomach had started jumping. She didn't want to see the deep gash again. Watching it bleed like it did when it happened was enough.

"I can finish for you. Just turn your head please just in the event that we're wrong about you. I know that you don't want to look at it so soon after it happened." She felt Mel gently remove the final layers and heard her hiss of breath.

"It's bad isn't it? I...I didn't realize the knife was so sharp when I was using it. And it went in so quickly that I didn't even feel the pain until just before I hit the floor." She still wasn't ready to look, but knew eventually she'd have to change the dressing herself.

"It's healed. There isn't even a scar. I thought as much." Mel sounded so smug that Maddy wanted to hit her.

"That can't be, I...oh shit, and it's gone. You can't even tell where I cut myself."

Maddy ran her hand experimentally over the area, the turned her arm over to check the other side. It really was gone, nothing there. When she looked down at the gauze she noticed little black threads caught in the material. It made her dizzy to realize that it was the stitches that the doctor had put in to hold the wound together.

"I think I'm gonna be sick..." She suddenly had her head between her legs, and was held there by one of the women.

"Breathe deep. I take it you've never done this before?" It was Mel's voice, but it might have been Savannah's as they sounded the same with the blood roaring through her ears.

"Passed out, cut myself or healed this fast? Because I gotta tell you," she said slightly panicky, "I can't think past those little black fuzziness."

Chapter Eighteen

Kyle woke around sunset and made ready to go to the hospital. They were releasing her tonight and he wanted everything perfect for her when he brought her home. He'd had Duncan pick her up several pies from Sam's Bakery and he'd also had him bring in fruit and juices. He wanted to keep her healthy.

He'd been pleased and surprised when she reached out to him this morning. He grinned when he thought of her reaction to the images he had sent her, the need she was feeling. He couldn't wait to get her home, and beneath him. And he wanted to complete their bond. His need for her to taste him, to drink from him was paramount.

He could hear Mel's laughter when he got off the elevator and then Madison's. His entire body reacted to the sound as if she'd stroked him. He'd never had such a reaction to a woman before and was still marveling at it when he opened the door to her room.

Every eye in the room turned to him, but he only saw her. Her cheeks were rosy and flushed; her hair was hanging down and mused. The hospital gown she had on was unbuttoned save one and her creamy shoulder and neck beckoned him, his mouth watered at the sight. He could hear her heart beating and felt his own pick up the pace when hers did. Even from across the room he could see the beating of her pulse at her neck.

Moving forward he nearly reached her and the bed when someone took the flowers from him. He'd forgotten all about them, he brought her daisies, colorful daisies.

"Hi. I didn't expect you…I mean I thought you'd have to…you know, have dinner." She looked away, her face red.

"No. I didn't. I came as soon as I could. They're letting you go tonight and I thought you'd need a ride home." He was flustered and unsure of himself. He was fourteen hundred years old for Christ's sake and was acting like a teenage boy.

"I was going to take her home. She has some things she needs to get from her friends, and then she's staying with us at the pack house for a few weeks." Kyle growled at Bradley. Bradley just grinned in return.

"Did you just growl at him? Oh grow up. He was kind enough to offer a place for me to stay. Why on earth would that make you mad at him?" She asked him.

"He knows. And you won't be staying at his house, or any others. You'll be coming back to the estate where Sara is." He folded his arms over his chest and glared at her.

"Sara is there because she lives there and in case it has escaped your notice, I don't. What the hell does that have to do with anything?" She couldn't be this dense he thought, he'd bet even Mac could figure it out.

"She's a woman, and the pack house has no bitch, so you won't be staying there without one." He glared at her harder to make his point but for some reason he felt he was failing. "I mean it Madison; you'll be coming back to the house with me tonight." He sat down in the chair and waited for her to comply.

"Oh I got news for you, you big headed jerk, no matter where I'm at there's gonna be a bitch." She got up from the bed and he stood up as well. She started poking him in the chest with her finger, hard. "I don't know who you think you are, or where you think you might have gotten the idea that you are in any way shape or form my lord and master, but you are not going—" He wasn't going to let her win in this.

"I am your mate and I will—"

"You will shut your fucking mouth while I'm talking," she shouted right back at him. "I have never...And you," She'd turned on Aaron so quickly Kyle thought he might be off the hook. "Don't you dare pretend that you aren't laughing. Coughing isn't covering anything." She turned back and picked up just where she'd left off with him. "You will get out of this room and you will not return, or so help me I will cut that impressive dick of yours off and plaster it to your forehead. That way everytime you look in the mirror, you'll see just was a dick head looks like. Mel, you said I could come to the castle. I've never seen a castle. I think it's time I visit one. Right now."

With a whirl of magic, both Mel and Maddy were gone. Kyle sat heavily down in the chair and rubbed his chest where she had poked him a good dozen times. He looked over at Aaron then at Sara. He felt like he'd be hit with a bat.

"That could have gone better." He hadn't meant to say it out loud, but it slipped out before his mind could censure it. Aaron's laughter only served to piss him off more. And when he looked to Sara for help, thinking as a woman who needed protecting she'd understand, but knew immediately that he'd find no help from that quarter. Her tears of laughter were streaming down her face faster than Aarons. "You people are nuts." He murmured as he got up and left the room. He could hear their laughter all the way down the hall.

~~~

The next morning at seven forty-five Maddy was in the downtown courthouse waiting for Danny to show up and her escort for the day. Mel had told her that she'd be better off taking the person to stay with her until they found out who was threatening her.

Her first official case on her own, and nervous did not even begin to cover how she was feeling. She'd gone over her case several times last night and had finally given up and took a walk around the realm. She'd been gone from the room about five minutes when she realized that she was in a place where no human need tread. She'd seen more creatures in that few minutes than she'd believed were real. She spent the rest of the night huddled under the covers in the massive bed she'd been given.

Maddy tugged at her skirt again, trying to bring it down to at least her mid thigh. When she had realized that she had nothing to wear today, Mel had suggested that she wear something of hers. They were about the same size and there were plenty of beings around that could handle a needle, a few who could fit into the little eye.

"Will you stop pulling at your clothes? You're going to look all rumbled if you keep that up. You look fine. Trust me." Mel said with a grin.

"I trusted you when you said that you'd have this altered in time to fit me. Silly me, I thought you were going to have it let out and lengthened not shortened to my who-haw and so tight I'm afraid to take a deep breath." Maddy tugged again.

The stupid thing was not moving down, but seemed to keep moving up. If this kept up she thought it'd be around her neck in no time.

"You look like a very chic young lawyer, and you should wear clothes like that more often. Are you even aware of the looks you're getting? You look stunning," Mel told her. Maddy had noticed.

"They are probably wondering how much I cost an hour." But Maddy had to admit, she did look good, despite the short skirt.

The skirt and little half jacket were made of silk and linen and of the most beautiful shade of lavender she'd ever seen. The jacket had three quarter sleeves, wide collar and two small buttons in the front. The buttons themselves were a work of art, ivory carved to look like small wild violets she picked in her yard as a child. The silk camisole was a deep, deep dark purple with the same small buttons around the scoop of the neck line that hung lovingly across her breasts. The skirt, while short had a tiny belt that just peaked below the jacket and was the same color as the camisole. The shoes were the thing she loved most about the outfit. The same color as the suit it featured the flower pattern over the top of her foot and along the strap that buckled them on her feet. The three inch heels were thin, but not dangerously so and made her legs look a mile long and her calf thick and strong. The thigh high stockings were sleek and felt decadent on her legs.

Maddy sat down again and fingered the beautiful bag that had come for her this morning before she'd left to come to the courthouse. It was a gift from her new bosses. They had decided on a name and B.A.C.K. Incorporated wanted to thank their new attorney in an appropriate way.

The leather satchel was dark brown and had a long strap and a pocket on the outside. But it was what was inside that surprised her even more. They had gotten her a laptop, and not just any laptop, but state of the art. It had a large hard-drive, CD burner and player, and was internet and Y-five ready. She fell in love with it and had played with it for nearly an hour before going to bed. The bag had also been filled with every lawyers needs, from yellow pads and pens, to a small digital recorder and calculator.

The appointment book was already marked with important dates, one of which had been circled in red marker. She had gone to see Mel to ask her about it last night.

"What's this date?" There was no entry, but just a time and an address, the MacManus address.

"Oh that's the twin's birthday party. It's in ink, you have to come now. Every good lawyer knows that." Mel had told her with a wink.

"Will you please stop pacing? You're going to wear a hole in the carpet. He'll be here soon and so will our guy." Mel had told her right before they'd left that she was Fae.

"And a full blood one too. How you got past my radar is beyond me." Mel had continued on.

The thing from her dreams he was a demon and a dream walker. And until they could determine who or what was helping him, she would need to be very careful and not be left alone until they caught the being that had been invading her dreams. When she had asked her why, Mel didn't know, not really. But she had a few ideas and wanted to talk to the Printer, a hired gun for the realm to see what they could find out.

"Also, Kyle is looking into it. He is by far the most tenacious investigator I've ever met. If there is information out there to be found, he'll find it."

Maddy wasn't sure what to think of a hired gun for the realm would entail. She'd thought that Mel being the queen and all she'd only have to zap someone to get rid of them. But apparently even queens had rules to follow. Before she could ask her again about the printer, Danny came running down the hall towards her.

"Hi. I'm sorry I'm late, I got hung up on a tyranny and couldn't seem to get it in straight, and then I couldn't get this ridiculous tie to work right. I'm telling...Christ Mad, you look fucking great! Sorry. Who knew you had legs that long, and shapely...could about make a faggot turn hetro really fast." Danny had finally made it with ten minutes to spare.

"Behave you old poop, you're just being nice. Now as soon as someone from the p...my bosses bodyguards get here so Mel can leave we'll be all set." Maddy was blushing a deep shade of crimson, but felt flattered by Danny's sincere words.

"I'm here. I'm here. Mel, how are you? You must be Danny March, I'm Bradley Wolff. I'll be hanging out with you for part of the day love. The one I had lined up hit a snag." Maddy just looked at him and when she started to question him about why he was there and not one of the other wolves her case was called and she needed to get inside.

"All raise this court in now in session. Mr. Button you will now state your case, and be quick about it, no preaching or postulating if you please." The Honorable Hamish Cornwell was a no nonsense judge and Maddy couldn't be happier with him being with her today.

"Your Honor, I'd like to state for the record that Ms Harm is being sued by my firm for breach of contract and would like to have a change of venue, if it pleases the court." Mr. Button said with a touch of impatience in his voice.

"You finally get away from these Jack wipes, Missy?" Hamish turned toward Maddy with a huge smile on his weathered face.

"Yes sir. I have moved on and up. It's amazing what an office with a window and eight hours a day can do for a girl's disposition." She had always had a cheeky relationship with

Hamish. She had loved clerking for him when she was in her second and third year of law. He'd also warned her not to go with Schaller and Schaller. Live and learn.

"Yeah, I'll just bet. Seems to have improved that wardrobe of yours a tad too. If you'd of dressed like that when you worked for me, you wouldn't have gone any further than my desk, as my law partner that is." He winked at her and turned to Button. "No, no change and no it does not please me. You never have you overblown excuse for a man. Now, state your case and try not to piss me off any more than you already have."

Bob blustered around and made it crystal clear that he had not been prepared to try this case, but to have had it thrown out on merit.

"Your Honor, I must in—"

"You do and it will be the last thing you insist on." Hamish picked up his gavel and banged it twice on the desk. "Proceed damn it."

Hamish Cornwall had been a judge for longer than either Bob or Maddy had been living and was due to retire soon. He was also a wolf and one in good standing in Bradley's pack or so Mel had told her.

Apparently when Bradley had called to tell him he'd be in the courthouse on Tuesday morning, "in case you see me around, I don't want you to worry," Hamish had asked him why. It didn't take him long to hunt down the assigned judge and have him trade sessions with him. His Honor hated Bob with as much passion as he loved the young Ms Harm Mel had told her with a huge grin.

"I will need a few minutes then, perhaps a recess until lunch? My second seems to have forgotten the file, err bring the right file." Bob was sweating. His very expensive suit was going to be ruined if he kept this up Maddy thought. Then she grinned. The stupid man might have looked around a bit before claiming that his 'second' forgot the file, as he was standing alone at the table.

"Wrong file you say? Ms Harm, I don't suppose you have an extra copy of the charges do you, for the Counselor and his…hummm, second chair?"

"No your Honor, I don't. Perhaps I can read my counter suit against Ms. Rosewood and that'll refresh his memory?" Maddy chanced a glance back to Bradley and was surprised to see both Kyle and Aaron with him.

"Doubtful, but let's give it a shot. He doesn't strike me as being overly bright, does he you?" Hamish looked back at Bob and sneered at him.

"Your Honor. Ms. Rosewood is claiming that my client Daniel March made unwanted sexual advances, lurid comments she found distasteful and demeaning and she further claims that he 'pressed her against her car and raped her repeatedly'. Maddy didn't have to refer to her notes, she had written the counter suit motion and literally knew it word for word.

"Does that ring any bells with you counselor? Although I must admit to being a bit confused, but hey if you don't do your homework then I guess you pay the price." Hamish winked at Maddy and she suddenly knew that he was aware of what had happened to Danny to make this claim impossible.

Danny was a teenager when his father had found out he was gay. The man had tried everything to get his son to "change his mind". But after several months of threats and hitting his son, Danny's father had taken a ball bat to him.

"Yes, that sounds about right your Honor. I have evidence to the fact that Ms Rosewood was brutalized by Mr. March when she came in to pick up her car. Mr. March allegedly told her that in return for her repair work on her car, he would take her body out in trade not money." He was still shuffling papers around on the desk, for what reason Maddy couldn't fathom, he had already claimed he'd forgotten the file.

"Your Honor, I have evidence and court records indicating that there is no way medically possible for Mr. March to have raped her, thus making the rest of her claim questionable." Maddy was walking to the judge's dais when she felt the hair on the back of her neck rise. She turned slowly and saw a figure, a blurry...something. It was only there for a second or two, then gone. Both Kyle and Aaron had stood and turned in the same direction, whether from her movement or because they too had felt the eerie feeling she didn't know.

"Yes, Ms Harm I'm aware of the evidence. Counselor, have you even done any homework on this case?"

"Yes your Honor, but as I have said, I do not have my notes in front of me, if I could have a brief—"

"Asked and answered. Proceed with your case. Bailiff."

Chapter Nineteen

The case started with very teary Ms Rosewood telling; in graphic detail what Mr. March had done to her when she had went to his place of business to pick up her car. She also went on to say that he had called her house repeatedly since then, demanding that she finish her bill off. She had just pulled out her industrial sized box of tissues and a note pad to read off dates of the alleged calls when someone tapped Maddy on the shoulder. She turned to have Kyle lean in and speak in her ear.

"That dress on you should be illegal, and if those stockings are thigh highs, you are *not* leaving this building unmolested." Then he just leaned back in his seat, looking for the all world as a bored man.

Maddy turned back around and stared blankly at the wall. Her whole body was on fire for him. When Danny poked her for the second time to get her attention, she was startled to remember where she was and blushed furiously, and turned around again to glare at Kyle.

"You're up Ms. Harm." The judge smiled at her and she just knew that the old coot knew exactly what she'd been musing about.

"Ms Rosewood," Maddy cleared her throat twice before she could continue. "You said that Mr. March raped you repeatedly, is that correct? And this was in his garage, his place of business."

"Yes," the woman sobbed. "He said that he had enough money and wanted him some...well, ladies don't speak of such things."

"Of course not. Enough money? Well that must be nice, to have enough money, I mean. Do you? Have enough money?" She had opened the door thought Maddy, and decided to go for it.

"What a rude question. I won't answer that." Ms. Rosewood squirmed around in her seat.

"The reason I'm asking is because three years ago you said that same thing about the owner of the dry cleaners on Seventh Street. Of course it isn't there now. I guess giving you five point seven million dollars in settlement meant he'd over exaggerated his lack of need for money a little. Then there's the antique dealer on Tenth from eight years ago. Of course that was only a mere three million. But cost of living and all."

"Your Honor," Button hopped up from his chair and nearly toppling it. "I don't know where Ms Harm is going with this, but bringing up Ms Rosewood's unfortunate past is uncalled for. She is a very beautiful woman and some men just won't take no for an answer."

"I wouldn't say nearly ten million dollars in less than ten years unfortunate. I could go back further your Honor, if you'd like. The 'unfortunate' Ms Rosewood, aka Rose, aka Wood, aka Woodrose has been bilking...sorry having men allegedly taking advantage of her for nearly twenty-five years, to the amount of forty three million five hundred dollars. That's an income of nearly two million per year. And, I believe, its tax free."

"You bitch. You make it sound as if I'm lying! Those men deserved what I did to them. Not a one of them paid me a second glance when I offered myself to them. Well I fixed them didn't I? All men are stupid and only think with their dicks." Ms. Rosewood had jumped up from her seat and threw her box of tissues at Maddy, narrowly missing her.

"Also your Honor, I have documented medical records stating that it is in fact impossible for Mr. March to have raped Ms. Rosewood, repeatedly or otherwise. He is—"

"I know what he did to me," Ms Rose screamed at Maddy, trembling with her anger. "He raped me, right there on the hood of my own car. Why it took me a new paint job to get the scratches off. I should charge him for that too. In fact, he wasn't all that good."

"Well I should say not. Mr. March can't have raped you Ms. Rosewood. It is physically impossible for him to of done so."

"What he couldn't get it up for you so you assume that it's because he can't get it up for anyone else? I got news for you honey I can get anyone to get it up. Even the biggest queer you know."

"As it happens, Mr. March is the biggest queer I know, and his dick as you so delicately put it won't get up for anyone. He doesn't have one."

Every man in the courtroom shifted in their seats and some even went so far as to hold themselves in a protective-like cup.

"According to this police record and these medical records, when Mr. March was seventeen years old he informed his parents that he was gay. Not a word widely used then but for sake of clarification it works. His father, a city worker for the water department decided that he'd 'beat this disease out of him' and took a baseball bat to Mr. March's private parts. The senior Mr. March beat his son so badly that the blood vessels in the groin and testicles were damaged." Maddy handed the judge the file she had as she continued. "The father refused to take Daniel to the hospital because he was convinced that they would ask the younger Mr. March why he'd been beaten and he would tell them his outlandish story about preferring men over women. When he didn't receive medical treatment right away, peritonitis set in and the infection was so severe that they had to not only remove his testicles, but eventually his penis and one kidney."

"No fucking way!" Bob exclaimed to Danny.

"Counselor! Your Honor, please? Hasn't my client suffered enough without Mr. Butt Hole, err Button making comments such as those." Maddy was appalled at him, Christ didn't the man have one decent bone in his body.

"In light of recent evidence," Maddy started to say, "I'd like to have the charges dropped against my client, and to also counter sue Ms Rosewood for defamation of character, then there's pain and suffering and—"

"Wait! You mean I'm not gonna get my money? Oh no, that *so* ain't gonna happen. He raped me and I deserve to be compensated for it. Bobby, you said I'd win hands down, that this bitch had never been to court and you'd have it slam-dunked by lunch. I rented us a nice hotel room at the Ritz." She stomped her foot. "I want my damned money."

"Ms Rosewood, where you are going is to jail. Filing a false claim and wasting mine and this courts time is against the law. Bailiff, take her away," Hamish said with humor.

They all watched in stunned silence as Delia Rosewood was flanked by two court room bailiffs to be escorted from the room. While one of them attempted to handcuff her, the other held her steady. When suddenly she broke free and made to attack Maddy. Danny leapt over the table and charged her, ramming his head into her left shoulder and knocking her to the floor, taking one of the men with her. This time when they tried to take her away, it was at gun point.

"Mr. Button, what am I to do with you," Hamish asked when the room was brought back under control with a few more bangs of his gavel.

"I had no idea your Honor. I'm just as shocked as you are. You can be assured that our law firm will help Mr. March in any way we can."

"I'm so glad to hear you say that, so glad indeed. Your law firm will pay damages in the tune of fifty million to Mr. March by end of business Friday."

"Fifty…fifty million? I meant with legal fees and such, not money, you misunder—"

"Read back what Mr. Button said for me, will you Sheila," Hamish said cutting off Button from what Maddy was sure was going to be a bunch of promises and some more lies.

"Yes sir, your Honor. '*I had no idea your Honor. I'm just as shocked as you are. You can be assured that our law firm will help Mr. March in any way we can.*' Is that all you need, sir?"

"Yes dear, thanks. I didn't hear any qualifiers in there, did you?" Maddy shook her head no when he pointed his gavel at her when he asked. "No, well fifty. By Friday, and don't make me have to come for it or else you'll be in hotter water than you are right now. Court adjourned."

Maddy sat down hard in her chair, and looked over at Danny. "I guess we won."

"Holy shit, girl," Danny said laughing. "I just wanted her to leave me alone, and you get me fifty million. Consider any and all car work done from now on free of charge. Damn girl." He got up then and walked to shake hands with Bradley. Maddy didn't move.

"Come with me love, now. We have some unfinished business to take care of." Kyle pulled her up from the seat and lacing his fingers with hers, pulled her along and out of the courtroom. With a curt 'watch her shit' to Aaron they were out the door.

He was pulling on door knobs and opening doors for a few minutes before she realized what he was doing.

"What are you looking for? Don't you have to be home in your crypt or something?"

"No, I don't sleep in a crypt, as you very well know." He kissed her quickly on the mouth. "I'm looking for an empty room. Now shush up, I don't want you to waste your energy. Ah ha!" He opened the small conference room door and pulled her in behind him. Before the lock was completely engaged, he had her pressed against the wall with his body and kissing her again.

~~~

Never losing contact with her mouth, he cupped her ass and picked Maddy up, her legs wrapping around his narrow hips. With her legs secured around him and locked at the ankles he ran his hands up her thighs to discover if she was indeed wearing thigh high stockings. His hands reached the top of them and he groaned in pleasure. He pulled his mouth away and nearly groaned again when she whimpered at him.

"I love these," he told her with his fingers just under the lace at the top. "Stockings with garters are sexy to begin with, but these just do things to me like nothing else can."

"Shall I take them off and leave the three of you alone? I can you know, Mel made me practice several time removing them." Maddy ran her fingers under the lace as well, teasing him. "She said it's an art form to take them off without tearing them. They're silk, pure silk, and they feel so sexy on my legs."

"Yes they do, very sexy. Unbutton your jacket for me? I want to see what other treasures you have hidden under there."

He watched her push each button through the tiny little hole, slowly so as not to snag the material she said. He pushed his cock against her core when she made to tantalize him with the final button getting 'hung up on the hole.' It suddenly freed itself.

His hands cupped her ass again, squeezing it and riding her up and down his shaft while she worked at the buttons on his shirt.

"You have too…Oh Kyle, I can't think when you…I can't get the…"

He kissed her again, his tongue sweeping inside her heat, the wet heat of her mouth and tasting her. He pulled the camisole up and over her head and his breath caught at the sight of the flimsy scrap of material holding those lush globes of flesh captive.

"Take it off." His voice was hard, gravely and deep. He was panting, his breath catching in his throat and making him slightly dizzy with need. Instead of taking the bra off she reached up and cupped her breasts, pushing them up and spilling them nearly out of the cups. Rubbing them hard, squeezing them together and then apart pushed him over the edge of sanity.

He dropped her legs, forcing her to stand on her wobbly feet. He fell to his knees before her and running his hand up the sides of the skirt, pushed it up and reveled her panties a couple of inches above where the hem line had been.

"Madison, look at me." When she did, he knew just what she was seeing. His eyes had turned, they were now a deep blood red, and his fangs had dropped lower than she'd ever seen them, at least an inch below his lip. "I'm going to eat you, eat your pussy until you come in my mouth over and over. Then I'm going to feed from you, I'm going to bite you deep on your pussy and feed from you."

"Please…I'm begging you, Kyle please. I…I want you to fuck me. Please, please hurry."

Biting into her panties and pulling them away from her body. He tore them in half, making her cry out and her knees nearly buckle. He held her up, not wanting anything to keep him from his feast.

"Don't fall, don't you dare fall." He spread her legs wider and pulled the swollen tiny nub of flesh into his mouth and suckled it.

She came, screaming his name she came hard and fast. Her hips bucked against his mouth as he suckled her. He inserted his finger into her dripping heat, then another. Her juices were running down his hand and along his forearm. Still he fucked her with his tongue and mouth, bringing her quickly to another then another peak. When she came the fourth time he struck, sinking his teeth deep into her femininity and drank. Her blood was hot, lava hot, first filling his mouth, then scorching his throat as he swallowed her down. When she came again from the bite, he lowered her to the floor, drinking deeply of her essences and blood.

Sealing the tiny punctures with his tongue, he sat up on his knees and unbuckled his belt and pants. His cock leapt free of its confines. He was dizzy with want and the taste of her blood. He fisted his cock, spreading the oozing juices of his own up and down himself.

"Madison, I need you, I need you to drink from me. I need it now. Will you? Will you take from me, be my mate?"

"Yes, oh yes now." She licked her lips as she watched him lengthened his nail on his hand and slice open the vein at his heart for her. His blood ran down his chest, over his flat male nipple toward his stomach. He positioned his cock at her entrance and picked her up and over him, pulling her down hard by her hips, he buried himself deep inside of her. She wasted no time and covered his wound with her mouth and drew her first taste of him into her.

Taking them both to the floor, he pumped into her, deep. He wanted it to last to feel her drawing from him longer, but her mouth and her heat proved too much and he came, bringing her with him again. He spilled his seed deep into her, over and over his cock jettisoned into her body. Not wanting to hurt her but needing to claim her he licked along the pulsing vein at her throat and bit, her essences filled him. He rolled to his back, he was spent and she lay limp and exhausted in his arms. He knew that he needed to leave the sun was nearly to the peak now. But leaving her especially after what they had just shared was too much to bear.

It was several minutes later when there was a hard knock at the door. Kyle reached out to see who and found Aaron and Colin just beyond. He knew they were reminding him, and he also knew as soon as they smelled her, they would know that they had truly bonded, mated for all eternity.

"Give us a few minutes, we'll be right there." He was reluctant to wake her, but he needed to get to shelter soon.

"I'm sorry old man, but it is nearly ten now, much longer and we'll need to find something closer to here. A good reason to find a house in town to renovate I think." He knew what Aaron was doing, he was letting Kyle tell him in his own way, and he was grateful to him.

"We've truly mated, bonded in the way of our people. I'm in love for the first time in my entire existence. Oh Christ Aaron, how will I make her happy?" His mind just caught up with what his heart had been telling him since he first met her, he was in love with Madison Shelby Harm.

"Making her happy will be much easier than you think, but if you're a crispy fritter, it will matter not. Move it in gear, I have a mate to please myself."

Kyle gently moved Maddy to her back and began to wake her. When she opened her eyes finally he smiled down at her, her returning smile was more than he could have hoped for.

"I have to leave, it's getting late. Come to the mansion today. I want you to stay with me, please? Stay with me for the day."

"I have to file with the courts and do some work to finish this case. But I will come by before you...I mean you know before you have to...eat?"

"You are my only source of food love, but I'll be fine tonight, with my age comes the ability to go for several days without feeding. You'll need to eat more and drink lots more though." He didn't want to bring up anything to sour the mood but had to tell her. "Maddy, we still need to talk about some things, all right."

After they both dressed, she agreed she would come there after she was finished in town. She was dismayed to realize that one of the stockings had torn, but he promised to replace them and wanted to see her in nothing but silk and thigh highs for the rest of their lives together.

"That isn't the least bit practical, but I promise we'll work something out," she told him with all the practicality that was his Maddy. With another scorching kiss, they opened the door.

"Welcome to my Kiss, Maddy. You are now truly a child of mine." Aaron hugged her tight, too tight as far as Kyle was concerned and Colin kissed her cheek.

"Just great! Well Daddy dearest, get my mate home before too much longer."

They left shortly after that and Maddy and her escort Eon, this one the pack member she'd been expecting this morning, went to file her win and to petition for the money from Schaller and Schaller for Danny.

Chapter Twenty

"Congrads, Miss Thing!! That had to feel good." Mary Smith had been filing at the court house forever it seemed and knew everything and everyone and their business.

"You have no idea. I guess we'll have to wait and see if they counter, or file yet. That's a great deal of money and you know Mr. Schaller. Mary, I'd like you to meet a friend of mine, Eon, Eon this is Mary Smith." Mary had told her that Schaller had moved out of his family home the year before he graduated from college and had set up housekeeping in a cheap apartment to establish himself an address other than home just so he could get as much government assistance as he could. Cheap did not do justice to Sherman Schaller.

"I know Eon, he and I hang out at the same kinda meetings don't we young man? Straighten up like I told you, never will get a girl hanging your head down between your legs."

"Yes ma'am. I was...we are...I'm escorting Ms Maddy today." Eon hadn't been with the pack long he'd told her, just a few years and until then, he'd not known he was a wolf. Maddy liked the young man and his painful shyness around her was sort of cute.

"Good for you. Escorting a pretty lady like Maddy is a good job to have. Don't let that big vamp scare you, he's a pussy cat. And don't you worry any about that with the money either," Mary told her. "Hamish already filed a lean against the business for midnight Friday. They'll pay or every payroll check they write will bounce. Wouldn't you just love it if they don't?"

"They'll probably charge each person the bounced check charge knowing those two."

After a few more minutes of exchanging gossip and wondering how someone so mean could be married to such and such, or about how ugly another person's baby was Maddy and Eon took off for her borrowed truck.

Just a few more weeks, she thought and my little baby will be running like a top. And to have Danny fixing it for life, well that might not be so long, it was over thirty years old. She really wouldn't hold him to that. He needed to make a living as well as anyone else.

She walked around the lot twice before she realized what she was doing. The truck wasn't there. She went back inside and retraced her step out again and still the truck wasn't where she thought she'd left it. She looked down the street.

"Maybe that guy Danny drove it home forgetting that he leant it to you." Eon had walked beside her every step of the way and never once complained.

"Ummm, maybe. But wouldn't he have noticed when he got back to the shop that my car was there? I'll have to find a payphone and give him a call." She didn't want to call him and tell him his car was gone, what if someone had taken it.

"I have a cell. You can use it." She took the phone and dialed the number to the shop. He did indeed have the truck, but he said that Kyle had told him to take it home that she wouldn't need it anymore.

"Well, did he tell you how I was supposed to get home without a car?" She was hot and frustrated and just a little embarrassed. She thought she knew why he hadn't told her, they had sort of gotten side tracked, but that didn't make her have a car.

"No, he didn't. I'm sorry Maddy. Carol, my assistant is coming into town now, I can have her pick you up with the truck and take you wherever you wanna go, okay?

"No, don't worry about it. I'll just get a cab. Thanks so much." She called the only cab company in town and made arrangements to be picked up. The lady said it would be a couple of hours. She handed the phone back to Eon and then the two of them went to the diner on the corner to eat lunch.

"Are you mad at him?" Eon was just finishing his fourth cheeseburger and third order of fries.

"Who, oh you mean Kyle? I don't know. It seems that one day I am the next I'm not." And she did too. Mostly it was mad, but after this morning, she was finding it harder and harder to stay angry.

"You're his mate now. I can smell him on you. It's strong, the scent."

She looked at Eon then flushed. "I don't know what to say to that. Other than sex, is there another smell you're talking about?" If he could be blunt so could she, she figured.

"Blood. But not just that, you give off a, don't know, a *back the fuck off I'm claimed* smell too. Other vamps, especially males would be able to know as soon as they were near you that you are claimed. It's the same with mated wolves too. You gonna eat that?"

She moved her plate over to him. He polished off her half eaten chicken sandwich in two bites.

"What does it smell like? I mean is it nasty and that's why they stay away?" This was the most information she'd had about this whole thing from anyone.

"No, the sex, the smell of…you're…you know, completion is arousing for us, all supers, I guess. But the mated smell, that's more primal, more earthy. So, is he not answering you?" Eon could change subjects almost faster than she could keep up. It took her a few seconds to catch up this time thinking about what he'd just told her.

"Answering me? I'm not sure what you mean." She must have looked really confused, because he laughed at her before answering.

"Alpha said that you hadn't been doing this for long. Kyle? Did you try reaching him telepathically yet?" He didn't have to talk to her like she was ten years old, she thought. Then it suddenly occurred to her what he meant. Of course!

"Oh my god, the mind melt thingy. I forgot about it." Closing her eyes, she pictured him in her mind, and formed the conversation to have with him.

"Kyle, Its Maddy Harm."

"I know love, I feel you when you talk to me. Did you miss me already?" She could feel his humor at her. Well how the heck was she supposed to know if it was her or not. It wasn't like she was calling him on the phone and caller id showed who was calling in.

"Miss you? No. Right now I'd like to smack you. Can you tell me where my car is?" She felt him then, the warmth and need he had for her.

"Your car? You don't… holy fuck! I didn't tell you! Shit baby, I'm so sorry. I was thinking about something…you know that's all I thought about since I left you. You sipped from me, drank from me. Do you have any idea what that me—"

"Focus Kyle, car! I had to call a cab to get around and poor Eon is eating me out of my next year's income."

"Car, right. We bought you one, a car. A company car, it's...fuck baby, its right there in the lot. It's the dark green Hummer. The keys, the security guard has them. You'll love it, it has GPS and voice activated everything. Honey, I'm so sorry."

"A new car? You guys bought me a new car? A Hummer. Let me go look at it, I'll call you...I'll hummm...let me touch you later."

"Oh baby. Fuck, I'm hard, don't tease me like that. You are always able to contact me, just say my name or think of me."

She got up and ran to the door. The waitress barely caught her before she darted out. She hastily paid the bill and left the restaurant. In her excitement she forgot all about Eon, but luckily he didn't forget her and stayed with her.

The Hummer was sitting right where he said it was. It was a smaller version of its older brother, and in a beautiful shade of forest green. She wanted to wait by the car while Eon went to retrieve the keys, but he made her come along with him. She skipped and hopped back and forth all the way in and out of the court house. After Eon opened the doors and checked it out, he handed her the keys. With a squeal of delight, she got in.

"I can feel your excitement. It's almost as good as being with you right now. So do you like it?" Kyle touched her gently not wanting to startle her again apparently.

"Are you nuts? It's beautiful, and so sexy. Where can I go, Oh," she thought excitedly. "I have to go to one of the sites, I have to meet Mr. Ontag there in twenty minutes, and I can use this GPS thingy too. Oh I love it! Are you coming with me?"

"No, you've worn me out today. And just in case you'd like a repeat performance tonight, I'll need to rest. You would wouldn't *you, like a repeat performance?"* Wave after wave of sexual heat washed through her, over her. She felt sexy and warm, soft and wet all at the same time.

"Oh you bet! I love you. Good night." She broke off the connection, not even realizing what she had said to him.

Maddy had been out at the site for nearly an hour with Mr. Ontag walking around one of the last three buildings that needed to be purchased when Eon walked over and handed her his cell phone and simply walked away.

"Hello, this is Madison Harm, may I help you?" She was confused, but she was also a professional.

"Ms Harm, this is David, David Wolff, there's been an accident. Can you come down to the hospital? Danny...Danny March is asking for you."

She could hear the hitch in his voice, and something else. He was emotional, but why she didn't know.

"Of course. What's happened? Can you tell me that much?" She walked over to her car, thinking to leave as soon as she could let the client know that something happened.

"Carol Martin, Danny's assistant and friend was killed this afternoon. Danny is taking it pretty hard. He asked me to give you a call, I hope that's okay."

"Yes, of course. I have to let my client know and I'll be right there. Oh, Eon is with me, is it all right if he comes as well?" She was shocked, first of all because David had said that she had been killed, and secondly because Danny had asked for her.

After letting Mr. Ontag know that she needed to go, she and Eon loaded up in the car and went to the hospital, thankfully not getting lost once.

As soon as they entered they were overwhelmed by the amount of people there. Danny saw her he came and engulfed her in a huge hug. She wasn't much of a touchy feely, but the hug felt good and she returned it with as much vigor as he gave.

"She called me," he sobbed in her neck. "While it was happening, she called me to tell me that someone was trying to run her off the road and that she didn't know who it was. She was my friend. I've known her my whole life. Why, why would anyone do such a thing to her?"

He was sobbing, and her heart hurt for him. His partner Russell was leaning against the wall looking like a man who had been pole axed.

That could very well have been me, she thought. If not for the new car, it would have been...Maddy had reached for the box of tissues on the table in front of her and froze.

"They ran her off the road? Where did this happen at?" Sitting back she looked at him, the box of tissues forgotten in her hand.

"Out on Washington, out near downtown, you know where that is," he asked taking the box from her hand. "She was running errands for me and the shop. She didn't know the car she said, her voice was so frantic. I had Russell call David on the cell, but he didn't make it. She was already dead when David got to her."

Maddy looked around the room, so many people and she knew so few of them, trusted even less of them. She'd been run off the road where she lived, on her street. What to do?

"Kyle, I'm so sorry, but I think I might be in trouble. And I don't know...you have to tell me who to trust." She tried to calm herself, tried to sound reasonable and in control.

"What Madison, what's going on? Where are you?" She could hear the worry in his voice, his was strained and hard. There was no joking or humor now.

"I'm at the hospital, with Danny and a lot of others. Carol Martin, the assistant for Danny's shop was run off the road today. She's dead, Kyle." She shuddered at the sound of it. *"I think it was meant for me. I should have been driving that truck, but you had Danny take it back. Carol was driving the truck that I should have been in. She was killed near my building on Washington Avenue. They killed her instead of me. Oh, Kyle..."*

"Okay honey, stay calm." Warmth and a feeling of complete security washed over her. *"You said there were a lot of other people there, who do you know?"*

"Eon, but he was with me, David Wolff, the cop, and Danny March. That's it. I'm so scared, what if I'm right?"

"Love, I'm going to have contact Aaron." He told her softly. *"You go to David, tell him just what you told me. I can't come to you, not for another couple of hours, baby. I want you to stay with David. All right? Don't leave his side."*

"You believe me? You believe that it might have been for me?" She didn't know whether to be happy about that or terrified, relieved that he didn't blow her off as some crackpot, or terrified that he believed someone wanted her dead.

"Yes. Of course. I'm going to go and find Aaron right now. Go to David. Tell him everything, okay? Stay with him, I know I keep saying that, but I need you to stay safe."

"Yes, I will. I'll find him now." She felt the open connection with him, the support and warmth coming through that connection.

David was with the family, Carol's family where taking her death understandably hard. She stood just out of sight, but close enough to keep David where she could see him. As soon as he stepped away, she gently touched his arm and gestured for him to follow her to an empty room.

"I think that that accident should have been me. I should have been driving the truck today but Kyle sent it back with Danny. They bought me a car you see, a company car and I really like it. It has GPS and a...and a..." She took a deep breath before continuing. "I'm babbling. I'm so sorry. I contacted Kyle with that mind thingy and he said to stay with you, to not to leave your side. I don't think he meant for me to follow you in the bathroom, do you? I'm doing it again, aren't I?" She sat down on the chair, sat down hard and burst into tears.

Chapter Twenty-One

"Maddy, honey, you have to calm down, all right?" David was sitting on the floor at her feet. He'd been there since she started crying.

"Calm down!! Are you insane!! Calm do…That woman was killed today and it should have been me. It might have been me. And you want me to calm down. I should bop you in the nose you idiot. Calm down." She was calming down despite the outburst, or maybe because of it. "I'm sorry."

"It's all right. It was a stupid thing to say to a hyst…to a beautiful woman such as you." He grinned at her.

"Good save fur ball. I was hysterical too. I'm so sorry. Kyle told me to find you and to stay close. Oh Captain Wolff, that poor girl died because of me."

"Why don't you tell me why you think that? I got that you got a new car. Congratulations on that, but why would that lead you to believe that someone wanted you dead?" He stood and went over to the rooms only other chair and sat down. It was then that she noticed that he had blood on his shirt and that it was torn in a few places.

"You were with her. You were…Danny said that he called you. I'm so sorry. You must have known her as well."

"It was horrible, I won't lie to you. She didn't suffer though. Tell me what you think Maddy, and please don't call me Captain Wolff. We're practically family."

She told him everything, even things that she hadn't had the chance to tell Kyle, the dreams, the room and with the hissing man. Then she told him about the car, and how she had supposed to have been to be driving it, that Kyle had made arrangements with Danny to take the truck, or she would have been driving it instead.

"I can see your concern and I think Kyle is right, I want you to stay with me until he can get here. I'll have someone stay with you during the day as well. I've already launched an investigation into Carol's murder, I'll see that it's stepped up a bit."

"There's something else. Hummm…it's my grandmother. She died a few months back. She was murdered too." She got up then and walked over to the window and looked out at the late afternoon sun. "She lived here in Ohio, I moved here just out of college to work. We were planning…She was planning to move into a house we'd worked on buying in a few months. Three months ago she called to tell me something, I can't remember what now. It's important though. Anyway, she called and told me it was dangerous, something was dangerous. The next day I got a call from the police. She'd been killed. Someone behind her hadn't stopped at a light and pushed her into the intersection into oncoming traffic. They said that it was a hit and run, that the person just, I don't know didn't have insurance or something and left the scene. It's never been solved." Her breath had formed condensation and she started making markings in it.

"Do you know who the investigating officer was, his name and the station?" He was watching her, still as the predator he was.

"Yeah, I talk to him about once or twice a month. It's Markus Ardmore. I think he's a captain. I have his phone number and badge number if that'll help."

"Okay, yeah, that will help. Maddy, you don't remember what your grandmother told you? She may have been giving you a clue as to what happened."

"Don't you think I know that? That I think about it every day? She's dead, she was everything to me and now she's gone." She walked back over to the chair and picked up her things. "I've told you everything I know and I'm hungry. If you're finished blaming me for her death, then I'd like to go to the cafeteria."

"Maddy, don't..." She turned and started out of the room but not before she looked back at the window.

"There's something there. Something I don't understand. I've been drawing it all my life and...Well, here lately it's gotten to be something I'm drawing all the time. Do you know what it is?"

David walked over to the window and blew on it. He turned back to her when he saw what it was. "It's a cross, one I haven't seen since I was a child. My grandmother had this old book...I don't know the title of it but she let us look at it. It's a Morrigan's cross."

She nodded. "But what does it mean?"

He told her he didn't know but he'd find out and let her know. David went out with her and into the outer room. She went to stand with Eon and Bradley, who must have shown up while she was talking to David. She shot David a look and walked from the room with the other two men. David was pulling out his cell phone when she walked away.

~~~

"So it was intent you think?" David had been talking with Markus for nearly twenty minutes and had found out a great deal about the accident, but very little about the woman who it happened to. It seemed that Ms. Heather Spring was a very nice older lady. That was it, nothing more. She didn't belong to any groups or clubs. She would be willing to help out with baked sales, but only as a buyer. She visited her granddaughter twice a month and stayed at the hotel. She had a driver's license, and blood donors card on her when she was killed, they were in her jeans pocket along with the name and phone number of Madison Harm on a scrap of paper.

"Yeah I do. But I don't know have any proof. The truck was a big black SUV with dark windows and it rammed into her going about sixty, she didn't stand a chance. Pushed her into the cross traffic and an oncoming semi going about seventy or so. Death was instantaneous."

"Did you find the truck, or the driver?" He had a feeling he knew the answer, but needed to ask anyway. Carol had told Danny that the vehicle that had been ramming her was a black SUV and had dark windows. The plates had been missing on the front, either because they'd been removed or it was from a state that didn't require them to be on both ends of the car.

"No to both. If you don't mind my asking, why are you interested? I mean that I understand that you know the granddaughter, but why the accident?"

"I have an unsolved accident here that involved a hit and run. The woman was run off the road allegedly by a black SUV as well. Maddy, Ms Harm told me about it and I thought I'd see what similarities there were."

"Was the woman, did she have a mark on her? A tattoo maybe?" David could hear the hesitation in the other man's voice, the uncertainty.

David felt his entire body chill and freeze up. He'd heard about the tattoo on Sara and Shade, and the markings that Pic and

Dominic carried all over their face and arms. They were markings of their race, species.

"What sort of markings?"

"This lady had a cross, a large cross on her back. It was beautiful, intricate in design with a gold circle at the cross. I had one of my guys look it up, it's a...let me see. Hang on. I'm gonna go pull the file." David waited, and waited. It seemed to be an eternity before he came back on the line. "It's a Morrigan's cross. Some sort of faerie queen or something, a goddess, can you believe that shit."

"Yeah, shit." David talked to him for a few minutes more then hung up. He sat back in the office chair and thought about all of this. Now what? He reached for the phone again and dialed a number as familiar as his own. "Hey Sara, it's David, what do you know about the Morrigan cross?"

David rode with Maddy to the mansion and Eon and Bradley followed in another car. She still wouldn't speak to him. She was still mad because she felt he'd been blaming her for the accident. Well, he hadn't. He'd tried to tell her that several times but she wouldn't even turn in his direction when he said her name. And shouting at her seemed to make her want to cry, so he stopped that and turned to look out the window. She'd been muttering to herself for the past ten minutes, knowing that he could probably hear her, but didn't care apparently.

"Stupid arrogant man, no not man, dog," she continued to mutter to herself. "A stupid arrogant dog. I'm going to insist that we put down papers in every room so he doesn't accidently piddle on the floor. Maybe the pee with short out his Taser gun thingy and shock his dick off. Would serve him right too."

"You do know that I can hear you, don't you? It's my special wolf ears, not dog, I'm a wolf. Maybe I'll just show you the difference when we get parked. And I don't think that you need—"

The rest of his statement was abruptly halted because of the seatbelt across his windpipe nearly tore his throat out. She had slammed on the brakes so hard that the locking mechanism locked up on the belts and with his forward motion, it cut into him. He looked over at her. Now he was not only quiet, he was fucking pissed.

With a little wave of apology to the car behind her and nearly on her bumper, she drove on with a big smile on her face. He looked over at her. She was enjoying herself. He would have laughed if he wasn't afraid she'd pull out the Taser gun and do just what she'd threatened to do to him.

Chapter Twenty-Two

Kyle and Aaron met them as they pulled in front of the big house, behind them stood the children, Sara and two women she'd never seen before. Maddy grabbed her bag and ran to met him. He picked her up in his arms and held her tight to him.

"Madison, oh Madison. Are you all right, love? Let me look at you." Kyle held her from him and touched her face, her arms, and then pulled her back to him. He kissed her then, devoured her mouth, her heat.

"You might wanna save that for later, we have a great deal to discuss. Kyle, did you hear me? I said to wait until later." Aaron poked Kyle hard in the shoulder, then a little harder in the back. When he finally got their attention, he grinned at them both.

"Fuck off Daddy dearest." And Maddy kissed Kyle again, thought not so intensely.

They adjourned into the house and into the big room with the massive fireplace. There was a fire tonight light in deference of the chill in the October night. The room was cozy and tight, and

Duncan had filled his tray with lots of goodies, some of which was pie. When Maddy saw the creamy slices she squealed with delight.

She was introduced to the other two women in the room, though she had already met one of them but wasn't sure until she spoke whether or not she'd remembered her. The other a Piccadilly Marshall, she didn't know her.

"Hello Ms Harm, it's nice to see you again." Shade looked so different that it had taken Maddy a few seconds to place where she'd met her. Then when she had she marveled at the difference in her appearance.

"Shade Doe! You look great. I can't believe it's you. And please call me Maddy. I'm so glad to hear about Brent. He must be getting so big by now. I read about you and the house you are running in the paper. I'm so happy for you both."

Maddy had been the court appointed lawyer for Shade when she had been accused of attacking a man in the apartment of Brenda Shell. Shade had gone there to feed the two small children that lived there, Brenda's children and got there just as a man by the name of Robert Peterson had murdered a little four year old girl by the name of Becca, Brent's sister. Brent had also been injured and at that time feared would die as well. But the paper had said that she and another man...Colin had adopted the little boy she remembered no.

The women promised to get together after the meeting tonight. And Maddy hoped that she and her would become friends. She seemed so less bossy than the other women in the room...namely Sara MacManus.

"I telled Aunt Sam to bring you some pie tonight. I thought you'd like it. There's more in the kitchen for later. I needs to talk with you Aunt Maddy, okay?" Mac had sat down on the couch next to her. Maddy leaned over and kissed him on the head and pulled him into her lap. She laughed out loud when Kyle made a face at the kid.

"I've wanted to talk to you too. I have something in the car for you and Lizzy. Ask your mom if you can have it now, or later." He took off like a shot and when permission was given, Kyle went out to her car and got the large box out of the back.

"I had these when I was little. I'm not sure where my Grammie got them, but she came home with them one day and said that I needed to keep them nice. She said I meet a little boy and a little girl one day and I was to give it to them." She was on the floor now with Mac and Lizzy on either side of her, opening the box and taking out the packing. First she pulled out a little box and handed it to Mac. "This is old, like I said I don't know where it came from, but it still works."

Mac opened the box slowly and sat back hard on his bottom when he looked inside. Reverently he pulled out a long gold chain, attached to it was pocket watch. The watch design was a wolf and a bat. The wolf was sitting on his haunches seemingly baying at the full moon, his canines long and sharp looking. The bat, flying across the moon was turned to the side and his fangs were fully extended. The carvings were deep into the gold and had darkened over time. Opening it carefully, music spilled out into the room, loud and clear. It was Beethoven's Fifth symphony, the notes perfect and in tune.

"Look on the back." And she helped him turn it over and when he read what was there he turned to his father and walked over to him and handed to him.

"It's yours, daddy. It has your name on the back of it, and a date." Mac sat up on his father's lap and watched as he stroked the watch, tears in his eyes.

"It's not...it wasn't mine. It was my fathers. I remember this. He wore it all the time and before he died...he...we had to sell it. It was made by a Bartholomew Manfredi during the fifteenth century." Aaron handed it back to his son. "The doctors wouldn't treat my father without money so my mother sold this to help. In the end it matter little. He died anyway, long before the doctor came around. We were very poor, you see. You say your Grammie found this?"

"Yes. She said that she just came across it. And I had it appraised it once, it worth a fortune, nearly three million dollars, but she said I couldn't sell it, that I would meet these two one day." Maddy turned to the box and starting taking out the rest of the packing and began talking to Lizzy. "I played with this more than the watch, really. I didn't want to ever put it up at night. She served me my first lemon meringue pie on it."

She handed Lizzy the first tea cup. Lizzy turned to her mother who came to sit beside her daughter. Then the tea pot, complete with handmade cozy was removed from the packing. Maddy kept handing her pieces as she unwrapped them and then to Sara when Lizzy's little hands filled with pottery. There were twenty five pieces in all, the pot with lid, sugar bowl and creamer both with lids, six cups, six saucers and six small plates. There was even a serving tray all made of fine porcelain. The design was the birth flower for October, three large yellow, red and orange marigolds hand-painted on the front, Lizzy's and Mac's birth month.

"Grammie made the cozy for it. It was all she could do really was to crochet some blankets and such and garden. She had beautiful gardens." Maddy wiped the tear from her eye and looked at the little girl." I hope you like it. I'll get you a fun gift later, I don't—"

Lizzy threw herself at Maddy, hugging her so tightly around the neck it was nearly impossible to breathe. Her tears streaming down her face blended with Maddy's as she returned the hug. They sat that way for perhaps five minutes until Mac came over and interrupted them.

"Let me hug her too. She gave me a gift too you know." Maddy laughed at his disgruntle tone and pulled Mac in with them.

"I don't want nothing else Aunt Maddy. That's the best present. Mom, can I show her, can I?" Lizzy ran from the room before getting her answer. She returned only a few minutes later with a big picture album. "This was my daddy's pictures. He said he didn't have many things left from when he was a kid, but these here pictures." She was turning the pages quickly. "Here! Look at this one." She turned the picture to Maddy.

It was Maddy's turn to be shocked. It was an old tin type, faded and worn at the edges with time and fingers touching it. There in the picture was a little boy and a little girl. It looked to be a small kitchen with a hearth fire going, they were in front of it. On the floor in front of them was the same tea set, complete with cozy and pie on two of the plates. She looked up at Sara, then at Aaron.

"It's my little sister and me. She had that tea set, Marie Jane. My sister had that same tea set when she was six. My mother took in laundry to pay for it, the watch too. She washed other people's clothes to get them for us for Christmas one year. I had a gun, a little toy gun, it shot little pellets. It was destroyed when our house was burnt to the ground some years later. Those were sold as I said for my father's physician and then for his funeral."

The children played with the small tea set for a while and the adults talked. When Maddy had finished her second slice of pie and laid back on the couch, Mac came and sat beside her and started eating a hunk of cake.

"I have to give you your message. I remember it all now. You have to let me tell you." Maddy nodded for him to continue.

"Your Grammie said I had to hurry. She said you have free willie and you should never forget that." Mac had his mouth full, but no one seemed to notice, especially Maddy.

"I'm sorry, did you say free willie?" She was slightly confused then it hit her. "Oh! You mean free will, well yes, everyone has free will. What else did she tell you?" After the past few days, Maddy was willing to believe anything, even a six year old.

"Yeah, she said she loves you very much, and that she's sorry she left you. Where did she leave you Aunt Maddy?"

Maddy thought about how to answer him, death was such a touchy subject for some people and she didn't know the MacManus' well enough to make any kind of statement concerning her grandmother death.

"Well, she passed on. Although, I'm not so sure she's actually passed on just yet. She left me when she died I guess. I miss her terribly and I loved her too. Would you mind telling her that next time you see her, that I love her too?"

"Of course I can do that. I like you Aunt Maddy. You're special." Then he laughed. He really was a cute kid she thought.

The kids were put to bed a little while later. Their treasures put in their rooms and marveled over again and again. Maddy kissed each of them good night and received another hug from them. She really liked them.

"David called me this afternoon, just after Carol's accident. He said that you and he had talked," Aaron said as they settled back down in the living room.

"Yes, but we argued more than talked, but okay. He...I think that the murder of Ms Martin was meant for me. I should have been driving that truck, and if you guys hadn't of gotten me one, I would have been."

"Why? I mean why do you think that? Is there something going on that you haven't told us? And does it have to do with the dreams at the hospital?" Kyle put his arm around her, pulled her close as he asked.

"The dream at the hospital wasn't the first time I've dreamt about this guy. He...I'm not even sure it's a guy, just an eerie feeling. Anyway, he comes to me and we're in this void with stale air. He hisses, all of his 's's all snaky like. And it says that I've been promised to him and that we are to breed lots of children, that the first will be his son."

"What do you mean void? And do you see him?" Pic asked. She had a very old and very large book in front of her with a laptop. She was making notes in the latter while she thumbed through the book.

"No, I've never seen him, like I said, I'm not even sure it's a guy. But the breeding part kinda makes me think it is. The void? Well, that's another weird feeling. It a completely white place, but not a room, a...void. I'm sorry, that's the best I can describe it. The air is stale and old smelling, as if it's been closed up for centuries and a breeze has never passed through." She felt ridiculous telling them of a bad dream, but thought that if telling it could make them go away then great.

"No, please you're doing great," Pic smiled encouragingly. "You can smell? Are you smelling the room then, or are you thinking that it smelled that way when you wake up?"

"Oh I see, did I add it later. Let me think...no, I smelled it when I was there. I remember thinking that at the time just how bad it was. The air, the second time, it was hot and hard to breathe. Then there's the pain, it horrible, just burning and searing." Maddy looked around the room. At first she thought they didn't believe her, and then she realized that they did. She wasn't sure which was more frightening.

"What does he say? Does he tell you why he's there, why now?" Pic was still making notes and had hardly looked up since she started.

"He told me his name if you want that." Maddy looked up from the glass she has just sat on the end table. The room had suddenly gotten quiet, deadly quiet.

"He told you his name? Maddy do you have any idea what it means to have his name," Sara said in awe. "No, I can see that you don't. There is great power in having a name. Has he ever used your name, your whole name?"

She thought for a few minutes, over each word that had been exchanged between them, what he had called her and what wording he had used.

"No. He's never used my name in any form, not even 'Maddy'. All he has called me is his love and ungrateful bitch. His name is Patcalus, but he pronounces it Patcalussss. He claims that I was promised to him, that all I need to do is tell...oh my god! Mac! Mac told me that I have free willies, err, free will. That's what she meant. I don't have to go to him, I can keep telling him no."

"You can keep telling him no, but it won't last for long. He'll tire of asking and just take what he wants. And when he does, he'll kill you for mating with someone else and your mate," a woman said. "Hello all. It's so nice to see you all."

Everyone in the room turned to look at the woman who had just suddenly materialized in the room. No one moved nor did they seem the least bit surprised to see her. Mel and her mother Savannah were just behind her, one on her right the other her left. Maddy looked at her hard and had a slight...memory or feeling she knew her.

"I know you...I...I remember you from somewhere? With my grandmother, but I...I was smaller." Maddy couldn't place her, her mind refused to let her remember fully. "You've not changed. You're very beautiful then and now."

"Thank you my child. I'm Morrigan, the Goddess of all Faeries. And you are the fair Madison Shelby Harm, direct descendant of mine, my seventh daughter of seven times seven."

"I don't think so. No, I have no family, no sisters. You're mistaken." Maddy began backing away from her, towards Kyle. Towards where she knew she would be safe.

"No, you were to be watched and cared for until such time that it was safe." The woman, the goddess walked toward her as she spoke. "It is nearly that time, Madison Shelby Harm, time for you to be released from the bonded of magic that has held you safe until now."

"Maybe you should sit down and tell us what you mean," Aaron stood up. Maddy felt the room expanded and suddenly knew it was magic. Strong and powerful it seemed to come alive in the room. She looked over at Aaron and knew that it was coming from him.

"Maddy, please sit with Kyle," Aaron said softly but with a bite of anger. "Mel, Savannah, you know how I feel about things like this brought to my home. I would very much appreciate it if when you bring magic into my home, you'd let me know in advance. Perhaps you'd like to explain this to us all?"

"I contacted Morrigan just after you told me about her grandmothers cross," Mel said with as much hostility in her voice. "It seems that Maddy has been missing since she was three. Her grandmother, the woman assigned to care for her was to leave her keep and never let anyone find them until Maddy reached the age of maturity." Mel motioned for Morrigan to have a seat and then took one herself.

"No, she was my grandmother," Maddy said. She didn't like where this was going. "You make her sound as if she was a sitter, she was more than that. Much, much more. I loved her."

"Of course you did." Morrigan went on to explain. "She had been caring for you since birth. There were twins born to your mother, you and your brother. You were born second, the seventh daughter of hers, as she was the seventh and so forth back. Your father, a man who fooled us all, killed your mother just after your brother was born. You should have died with her, still in the womb, but you were birthed, whisked away and hidden with a spell to keep you safe."

"But I don't understand. Why? Why now? Why did I need to be hidden, who cares what happened back then?" She let Kyle put his arms around her glad for the comfort.

"Because I have been waiting for you for millenniums, Madison Shelby Harm, you are the hope of all fairies, the next in line to take my place. On the date of your majority, you will become all, be all that I am and more. You must make a choice, the right choice to come with me, it's time to—"

"No," she shouted. "No, I don't want to be whatever. I want you to go, I want...there's been a mistake. You've got the wrong person. I'm just me, nothing special."

She was panicking, she could feel her heart pounding, her head was light and she felt dizzy. She was afraid too. Afraid that what these people were telling her was true, that she'd been taken away from her family because they'd been—

"You bear my mark, Madison Shelby H—"

"Stop calling me that," Maddy shouted again. "I'm just Maddy. I'm nobody. And you're wrong. I don't have a mark, not even a birth mark. You've got the wrong person."

"She doesn't have a mark. I've seen her, her skin is flawless." Kyle held her tighter now, and she could feel his comfort like it was a favorite shirt, worn jeans and comfy socks.

Morrigan reached forward and said, "If you believe that I have the wrong girl, then you'll let me touch you. Once I do, the mark that I have given you through your mother will show itself or it won't. If it does not then you are correct, and I have the wrong woman. But if it does then you'll let me explain, all right?"

Maddy looked at the outstretched hand, inches from her arm. She looked over her shoulder to Kyle and searched his face for a clue what to do. There was nothing, he was leaving this up to her. She looked back at the woman who held the key to everything she was and would be or nothing but a mistake. She nodded once and felt the hand close over her arm.

Flashes of her life passed in seconds. Her birth was first. The pain of it, struggling to live while the woman who had carried her inside of her breathed no more. Her flight in a warm blanket, bundled in someone's arms, tight and close. Learning to walk, and then run. Climbing the tree in front of a small cottage where she had fallen and broken her arm. The lessons on how not to bring attention to herself, and then college going into law instead of majoring in general fine arts as her grandmother wanted, and her disappointment. The dreams, she'd had them as a child too, many times she would wake up screaming and crying to be comforted by Grammie. All of this passed in seconds, each hitting her mind like a slap.

The burning began next, the searing pain in her shoulder. She didn't have to look or to be told what it meant. It was the mark, the mark Morrigan had told her she had. The one her Grammie told her was there, but wasn't to ever be talked about.

"Maddy? Are you all right?" Sara had come forward. "Maddy, honey, are you all right? I can feel your magic now. Please. Please tell me your al—"

"I'm...I think I'm gonna be sick." She jumped up and with her hand over her mouth ran to the bathroom. After closing and locking the door she sat in front of the toilet and threw up everything on her belly, then the dry heaves began, leaving her weak and drained. Once they subsided she lay on the cool tile floor and rested. She couldn't think, didn't want to, she just laid there.

"Madison, honey, are you all right? Let me in, I need to see you." He had gently entered her mind, but she could still feel him close, maybe as close as the bathroom door. She didn't have the energy to look and see, much less let him in.

"I'm all right. I've just had...I'm all right, I just need a few more minutes. Tell her she was right, the mark is over my right shoulder, I can feel it now." She could still feel him close, and wanted to let him in, to have him hold her, but she knew if she did that, she'd fall apart, so she just waited. *"I'm sorry Kyle. I swear to you I didn't know."*

"Baby, do you think I care? I love you, Madison. I need you. Please believe that. I'm here for you, everyone is here for you."

He would be too she thought, no matter what because he needed her. Didn't he tell her before that now that they had mated, bonded completely, he couldn't feed from anyone else, he'd die without her? She was his food.

She needed to get away, she needed to think. Looking around the tiny room she spied a small window and wondered if the fall would kill her and worse yet, did she care if it did. Standing as quietly as she could she opened the window and peered out, then down. She just had to come up to the second floor didn't she?

Taking a deep breath she threw her legs over the sill and sat there for a few seconds then dropped. It seemed to take forever, but as soon as she hit the ground she rolled and tumbled as she had been taught in self-defense classes. She lay there for a full minute trying to catch her breath and take a quick inventory of her body. She was fine, but she would probably be sore tomorrow. She stood up and keeping out of the window light, ran to the wooded area behind the house.

She'd been running for about ten minutes when she realized they could probably track her. Hadn't she read somewhere about how once a vampire took your blood they could follow you everywhere.

"Shit, shit, and double shit!" *Oh well*, she thought, *no help for it now* and she kept running. When she'd got to the high fence she nearly sobbed with relief until she realized the stupid thing was humming. Electricity ran through it, and according to the little sign she found just before she threw a stick at it to test it, there were one hundred and twenty thousand volts going through it. Even she knew that would probably sting just a little, "Well duh, you think?"

The forest suddenly got very still, no birds, insects or leaves were making any sound. That's when she heard the noise. It was large, very large and coming at her fast. The hair on the back of her neck and on her arms stood and her skin prickled. She thought about hiding, running again, but couldn't make her feet move. It was as if they were stuck to the ground. She turned her head around slowly and faced whatever it was, ready to be run down, or rescued. She could almost hope it was a rescue.

It stopped just out of her line of sight, but she knew deep within her heart that it wasn't Kyle or any of the rest of them. It seems Patcalus had come, he had waited long enough.

"Hello my dear, I've come for you, you are minessss. You will alwayssss be mine." She fainted just before he got close enough for her to see him. A black void swallowed her up.

Chapter Twenty-Three

Kyle had felt her leave the bathroom, he didn't get alarmed, he knew that the grounds were well covered and there were wolf pack always roaming the area. He left the mansion just as she had reached the forest, thinking to give her time to cool off. A lot had been thrown at her and she would need time to adjust, to take it all in. It was when she got scared that he began to run, her fear pouring into him as though it were his own.

"Aaron, she's…Something's wrong. She's afraid, something is chasing her. I can't get her to open to me, help me."

Kyle knew that Aaron would come and bring the others; he only hoped it wasn't too late. When she lost conciseness, he stopped cold, he had felt no pain, only terror, absolute terror.

Scenting the air he found her and followed it. Before he got much further than ten feet, he scented the wolf, and then another. They weren't pack, but wild animals. Wild animals not from the pack he'd come to know. These had been tainted with magic, black magic.

They attacked him as one. He had nearly overcome them both when two more joined them and they took him down. Tearing and pulling at his body they overpowered Kyle and held him immobile. He thought they'd kill him but they didn't they simply waited.

Kyle couldn't move. The larger wolf was at his throat, teeth and canines deep in the flesh. Two others held his wrist in the same manner, their teeth deep into the skin, just a small nip from tearing out the vein and the precious blood pumping through there. He needed to contact Aaron, to warn him.

"Hello vamp." The man leaned over to where Kyle could see him. "I see my animals have found something for dinner. I wouldn't move around too much. They are under the impression that to kill you would be a feast."

The man was huge, Kyle thought, bigger than him by a good thirty pounds and two inches. When the man grabbed his chin and jerked his face first one way then the other Kyle had the impression of insanity though where that thought had come from was anyone's guess.

"Ah, the mate. Good." The man reached behind him and that's when Kyle saw the blade seconds before he plunged it into his chest. Before he slipped completely away, he heard him say "Bring him."

Kyle woke in a room lying on what felt like a tilted table. He was weak and bleeding, the blade, he could tell that it was silver now, was still imbedded into his chest. His wrist and legs were strapped to the table with silver bands. When he moved his leg, the pain told him that there were more wounds there as well. He was being bled. Bled slowly and soon, with the blades and the wounds he'd be dead.

He looked around the room trying to see into the darkened corners and could see that nothing was there. He couldn't see behind him, but could hear a faint of panting sound behind him. Reaching out mentally he found that one of the wolves were in the room with him, but nothing else. Reaching further he hit a wall. If there was anything beyond the immediate room, Kyle couldn't penetrate it. Trying again and failing he figured he was in a lead room.

He thought of Maddy and where she could be. He hoped that she was still on the grounds, that someone had found her and she was now inside, safe. But he kept coming back to the comment made just before he blacked out, *'the mate'*. Whoever took him knew that he was Maddy's mate.

"Yes I do," the large man said just as a door opened behind him. "But you won't be for much longer. I plan to have her and let you watch while I do. You should not have taken what didn't belong to you vamp. She was promised to me."

"Fuck you. She's my mate and has been since the fates made it so." Brave words he thought. Now if only he could get up and take care of the man.

"Fate has nothing to do with this. She will be my breed mare, and have me my son. He will be the strongest being alive," he snarled at Kyle with a twist of the silver blade. "With her pure magic and my black, my child will have so much power we will be able to rule all kingdoms. We will rule the worlds he and I, in this realm and beyond."

"Where is she? What have you done with her? I want to see her right now." Kyle jerked against his bonds, tearing and opening the wounds, making them bleed more, the blood flow stronger.

"Demands? Demands lying as you are?" The man threw back his head and laughed without mirth, it was cold and harsh. Kyle saw the wolf in the corner pull himself tighter against the wall and whimper. "I will show you my mate because I deem it so, not you. She has proven...difficult. I've had to put her in her place. So don't be alarmed by the blood. She'll learn to do as I say or she'll get much worst."

The man walked over to the wall at the end of Kyle's feet and pushed against something. Kyle heard something heavy slide and the room brightened considerably. The man was at his head before the sliding mechanism was completely still. He jerked Kyle's head up by his hair and pushed him forward.

"She can't hear you," he whispered in Kyle's ear. "But if you'd like I can let you hear her. Her whimpering and simpering is quite nerve wracking, if you ask me." He reached down and pushed another button and sound filled the room.

She was crying, sobbing really. Kyle could see she was covered in blood. Her clothes were torn nearly off of her.

Maddy had been chained to the ceiling of the room, her arms pulled tight up over her head. There was another chain around her waist that held her to the wall, her legs were spread and shackled to the floor by leather straps that had cut into her skin, blood pooling at her feet. By some command that Kyle could not hear, a man stepped forward. A man Kyle knew. Robert Button was in the room with Maddy, and he was in league with the monster. He yanked Maddy's head up and pointed it to the window so that the man and Kyle had a full view of the damage done to her face.

She had been beaten, and beaten badly. Even through the window, Kyle could see that her nose was broken as was her left cheek shattered. Her left eye was hanging out of the socket and blood still poured from the gaping wound. Her jaw was also broken, the mandible hanging lax and without purpose. Her ear was nearly torn from her head. Kyle's heart hurt, his true love was so badly hurt and there was nothing he could do.

"Oh baby, oh my poor baby," Kyle sobbed. "Why? Why would you do this to her? She's done nothing wrong."

Kyle could feel the tears on his own face. He tried to break free of his bonds but all he managed to do was tear at his body, the silver making digging into his muscle and bone. Kyle's heart breaking for her.

"Why? Because she refuses me, the ungrateful bitch. Keeps talking about free willies or some other such nonsense. I don't want to have to rape her, taint our sons conception, but I will if she doesn't give in soon. Once she is carrying my seed, then I will let her heal long enough to deliver. But, I can't wait much longer, she is ripe now. I will not be put off." He dropped Kyle's head and he immediately felt the darkness swallowing him up.

He woke again sometime later, weaker than he had been in his entire life. He wasn't going to live much longer with the silver in him and without blood to repair the damage. His first thought, however was of Maddy and if she had given in or had she died. He hoped that she would have given in. He would rather see her live then dead. She could survive without him, but he could not without her didn't want to live without her actually. He knew that without her blood, he would die and if she was, then he didn't care anyway.

"There you are" the man said as soon as Kyle opened his eyes. "I thought you'd never wake this time. I have a surprise for you vamp, the lovely and damaged mate"

The wall between them was open, he could see her clearly now and Kyle could feel her weakness sharp. But the man was talking again, he voice sounded so reasonable, like he was used to getting what he wanted.

"You will make her give in to me, or I'll hurt her while you lay there watching. She is too stubborn for her own good. Now, tell her, tell her to give me what I want, or I swear I'll hurt her again." He grabbed her hair and yanked her head up. "Tell her vamp. Tell her to do what I say."

"Mad…" Kyle started to beg her to give him what he wanted but he felt her in his mind. She moved without thought to being gentle but with urgency.

"Don't! Don't say my name. Without our names, he has no power."

Before Kyle could respond to her the man back handed her, blood poured from the already broken skin of her face.

"You will not give him advice," he told her calmly. "If you do that again, I will simply kill him, rape you and have done with it. I am sorely tempted to take you here and now as he watches, but I don't want to have to do that. You will give in to me girl, give into me or he will die." Kyle noticed that Maddy wasn't listening, that with the blow he had rendered her unconscious again.

Listening deep he could tell that her heart was slow, and that soon, very soon it would stop altogether. Her breaths were shallow and fast, panting almost. He could also tell that she had all but two ribs broken and that her kidneys and liver had been abused so badly that they had shut down. Her legs and both of her arms had also been broken. Kyle could feel her will to live slipping away as quickly as her life was.

He needed to save her, reaching into her mind, he found a small spark and touched it, tried to stoke it as one would a spark to a flame.

"Love, call for her. Call for her to come to you. Please baby, call for her." Kyle felt the second blade slide into him before his saw it, then the third and fourth. The man was killing him. *"Call for her love, I'm dying anyway."* And he slipped away again.

196

Chapter Twenty-Four

Maddy was hanging again, her body in so much pain it was if there was nothing else. Moving her toes into the wet dirt beneath her, she realized that it was her blood making it dark, not the dirt itself.

Kyle. He was dying and she couldn't save him. He had told her to call her, who she couldn't remember. The pain was making everything fuzzy and out of focus. Who should she call? Ghostbusters, she thought and starting humming the song in her head.

The next time she woke she knew she wasn't alone, that Kyle was in the room with her, but he like her was near death. With sudden clarity she knew, that was who she needed to call. Morrigan.

When she tried to form the words, she nearly fainted from the pain in her face. She thought that now that she could remember she was too broken to call for her. Instead of giving up, she closed her eyes, at least she thought she did and thought of the woman in the house, pictured her face and clothes. Tried to remember what she smelled like and sounded like, and then she thought her name, shouted it through her mind.

"Morrigan, goddess of all Faeries, please come to me."
Maddy slipped once again into the welcoming darkness.

"You must wake my child. It's time to wake up." The voice was gentle and soft, not like her Grammies. But Maddy was tired, so tired and she didn't want to go to school today, she thought if she just slept a bit longer she'd…

"No, not today. I don't want to go to school today. Let me sleep." Maddy formed the words in her head knowing something was wrong, something would cause her pain if she tried to speak.

"Wake please love, you are running out of time. You called for me, now wake up and ask me, Madison Shelby Harm, ask me what you will of me."

Maddy's mind snapped awake. She had asked Morrigan to come and she had. Hopefully not too late, not too late for life.

"Does he live, my mate, does he live?" She didn't want to give the creature any more power over them but she needed to know if her mate still lived.

"Yes, just barely as do you. You must ask me Madison, you must ask me soon. Your breaths are nearly gone as is your life. Ask me what you will."

"Madison, love, you must live. Promise me…promise me that you will live. I cannot live without you, but you can without me. Promise me that you will live." Kyle's voice was weak and thready even in her mind. She knew they didn't have much time.

"He must live at all costs. Kyle Shane Dixon must live at all costs. I will die, but he must live on. Promise me this, Morrigan, goddess of the Faeries. He must live for me." Maddy slumped down, her body spent, her last breath just ready to leave her body. With it she uttered her last words, the words to set them free, *"I will love you forever Kyle Shane Dixon, mate of my heart."*

"No!" Kyle screamed into the room.

Suddenly the room brightened no shadows to be found in any corner. Morrigan reached out and cupped the breath of the child of seven times seven and whispered gently into it. She leaned over to Kyle and touched it to his lips, then dipped it into his blood. Turning back to the woman hanging there without life she chanted a song in a language Kyle thought long dead.

When she was finished, Morrigan once again walked over to the table that held Kyle and pulled each blade from his body, sealing the wound as she went. He didn't feel the pain, so focused on Maddy. He did feel the energy that poured into him but didn't really think about it.

"You must save her, I cannot live without her" Kyle begged her. "I have no reason to live without her. She is my everything, my all. Please, take my blood. It will save her, please, I beg of you."

Stopping for a moment she looked him straight in the eye, and told him the horrific truth. "She lives no longer, Madison Shelby Harm is dead. Come, it is time for us to leave. Bring her body and we will leave."

Kyle staggered to the wall where she hung and fell to her feet, sobbing for his one true love. Madison was dead. He could feel is as if it were his own death. Her skin was cool, her breaths no more. He couldn't even feel the faintest heart beat, she was indeed dead. Kyle wanted desperately to join her.

He was able to undo the chains about her with the help of Morrigan and soon he was cradling her broken body next to his. He walked outside the chamber where they had been taken and fell to the floor in her life's blood and sobbed for the woman and the pain she had endured. He sobbed for all that she was, and could have been.

"I have no wish to live, Morrigan. I cannot anyway. She was my life blood, I cannot survive without her. I don't even want to. As soon as she is buried, I will meet the sun. You should know this now. I will not go on without her."

Morrigan jerked around so fast he nearly dropped his precious burden. She was upon him so quickly he was hard against the wall before he could think to move.

"You will have her death mean nothing? You will let her sacrifice to save you be for nothing? You fool! You do not deserve her. Her last breath, her last thought was for you, for you to live, and by all that is magic you will, do you understand me, you will."

She turned back around and walked on, he could do nothing but follow her from the deep caverns.

Once they were out of the caves and onto green grass and under the full moon she had him lay Maddy onto the ground. He did so, reverently smoothing out her tattered clothing and wiping her hair from her battered face.

Raising her arms above her head, Morrigan started chanting again. Her voice was clear and strong, she called for her sisters seven.

"I beseech thee; sister's mine, to come to me now. I beseech thee, for the one who would lead us all. Come to me and heal her now, come to me and let her live. I beseech thee; sister's mine, to come to me now."

She repeated this twice more, then sat at the foot of Maddy's body and waited with her head bowed low. When Kyle started to speak, he heard the thunder roll in, rumbling and bowling across the sky. Then the earth moved, it shifted and danced beneath his feet as he stood to protect Maddy's body from the rain. Next came the lightening, streaking across the sky in bold strikes, hitting the earth were they stood.

And just as quickly as it rolled in, there were three women standing before him. One as black as the night, another in white as the lightening, the last as green as the grass.

"Kyle Shane Dixon, meet Mother Nature."

Chapter Twenty-Five

"Oh don't be so dramatic," the one in white said. "You always were one for the flare. I can't believe that you've not changed in all these millennium. We aren't Mother Nature, my dear boy, we are the Fates. I swear Morrigan. I don't know what to do with you sometimes."

"The Fates. *The* Fates. Right and I'm Saint Nick. Morrigan, what's going on? Let me take her home." Kyle leaned down to pick Maddy up but was stayed by a hand on his arm.

"We are the Fates Kyle, we've come to finish Madison's destiny. And yours if you answer correctly." Fate-One, the one in white kneeled down at Maddy's head, Fate-Two, the one in black at her left, Fate-Three, in all green at her right. They motioned Kyle at her feet.

"I know what you're thinking, we can't be the Fates," the one in white said to Kyle with a wink. "Well the books and movies have it all wrong, young man. Sharing an eye? Can you image how unsanitary that would be, one of us holding it out so the three of us can see? Nasty business. Then there is the whole short, fat and ugly hag routine. Do we look, short, fat or ugly to you? W*e do not!*"

Green Fate pulled things from her pockets as she talked. The other three women did the same, including Morrigan.

"And we don't even get along, not once in all these years. That's why we have to be called together, and we make such a racket. We have to try and outdo each other when we make an entrance." Black Fate was putting Maddy back together and when Kyle made to stop her she smacked his hand away.

"Please, just leave her be, I want to take her home with me." He made to pick her up again and Green Fate stopped him. "I don't know why you're here, and frankly I don't care, no offence, but I just wanna take my beloved home."

"We're here to save her. She is the future for us all. Tell us her name and well bring her back to you. Her full name."

Kyle looked at each woman in turn. He wanted to believe them, he did. But Maddy was dead. Bringing her back was not an option. He thought these women to be cruel, cruel beyond bearing.

"You're right Kyle, bringing her back is not an option. And we're not being anything but helpful," Morrigan nodded her head at him as she spoke. "You must give them a name Kyle. Give it to them and they will give this woman life."

"Her name? You'd like a name to bring this woman back? I don't understand any of this. What happened to that man? What happened to Button?" His head was spinning.

They were asking him something, asking him for something that he didn't know the answer to even though he knew that it was important. Fate-One had said he must answer correctly, if he did she'd come back. What did she mean?

He stared down at Maddy and thought about all the time they had missed out on fighting. His stupidity mostly, keeping them apart. He loved her and wanted to spend the rest of his lives with her as his mate, to have children with her, to drink from her, and have her drink from him.

With a clarity that overwhelmed him he knew what they asked, "Her name is Madison Shelby Dixon, my mate."

"Good boy," White fate said excitedly. "Now stand back and watch us work. Give us her breath Morrigan and the knife. Kyle my boy, you must do as I tell you and nothing more or nothing less, understand?" He nodded.

She was in full charge now he could see. He had a moment of terror when she reached into the sky but when only the wind blew softly he felt better. The four women started to glow, their bodies were glowing brightly in the night sky.

"Take this knife and cut your wrist when I tell you to. Cut it in an 'x' across the wrist where the vein is closest to the skin," she told him showing him just where to make the cut. "Then you'll need to tell this woman her name. You'll need to tell her that you give her this blood for her life, all right?"

"Yes, I understand. My blood for her life. Yes." He kept murmuring it under his breath and waiting for the signal.

"Ah, it was used in love," the woman said when Morrigan handed her the small orb of blue light. "Her last breath was used in love. Very poetic, yes very nice indeed."

They worked on his Maddy for ten minutes, chanting and touching her. Kyle watched their every move. When Black Fate nodded to him, he leaned up and cut his wrist deep just as he'd been told.

When she took his arm and laid it across Maddy's mouth he said in a clear voice, "Madison Shelby Dixon, I give my blood for your life."

Nothing happened for several seconds. Kyle didn't dare breathe and no one moved in the little circle surrounding Maddy. Then suddenly she took a small taste, then another. After about three deep draws from him he saw her chest rise and fall with breath, still he held his own. He looked to the Fates and when White Fate smiled at him then winked, he drew a deep breath himself.

"You have done well grasshopper," Green Fate said.

For about ten seconds no one moved, and then the three fates burst out laughing. "You should have seen your face, it was priceless," one of them said hilarity still evident in her voice. They continued to roar with laughter until Maddy moved.

"Hello my dear, how are you?" White Fate had been watching the closest, next to Kyle. She seemed to be waiting for her to wake.

"Kyle! Where's Kyle? Morrigan said she'd save him...Kyle?" She started thrashing around and trying to sit up, but Green Fate held her down.

"You're still a bit weak child. Just rest here for a bit longer. Kyle, please be a dear and come closer so that she can see you."

"I'm here, love, right here." He moved up to her face so that she would stop moving and rest as they'd said.

He had to touch her he realized and reached tentatively to do so. Her skin was warm and soft, and leaned in to kiss her cheek. Her fingers brushed against his cheek and he moved his face closer to her.

"I thought you were dead. I thought he had killed you. He said that you were to watch and then he'd kill you." He pulled her into his arms and held her close to him.

He looked down at her face and noticed for the first time that she was healing. Her eye had been put back in its socket before he'd fed her and was now staring up at him without any apparent damage to it. The bruises and lacerations along her cheeks were pink, but those too were fading as he watched. Her arms and legs also looked to be whole and mending. He wondered what sort of magic could do so much in so little time.

"The magic we used was secondary to her healing process," Morrigan said softly to his unasked question. "Your blood, it's mostly your blood. Given freely and with love it has healed her more quickly than we could. In a day or two she'll be completely healed."

"Perfect timing if I do say so myself!" The man from the sublevels had come up behind them and now had jerked Kyle back and had a blade to his throat. "Put her down and lean back away from her. You, bitch, move back. I'll kill him if you don't."

The Fate's and Morrigan moved away as they'd been told. Just as they raised their hands in unison, Kyle shook his head. This fucker was his.

"You won't take her from me again. I won't let you or anyone else try and separate us again. In fact, you'll not leave this clearing." Kyle hadn't moved an inch after laying Maddy back down on the grass. He knew she was too weak to fight and he was going to protect her at all costs.

"You think not," the man snarled, spittle spraying on Kyle's face. "She was promised to me bloodsucker, and I'll have her. She'll breed me a son, and then if I'm happy maybe I'll let her live, but first I'm going to fuck her until she is fat with my seed."

"You know, you keep saying that I was promised to you," Maddy said as she scooted away from them. "How and by who? I have a right to know before my mate kills you don't you think? Because for as much as this has been fun, I think you've more than outstayed your welcome, buck-o."

"Oh so brave aren't you. All right, I'll tell you. By who? Seems a reasonable enough question. Our daddy gave you to me. He said that I was meant to be the seventh times seven, and granted all the powers you'll receive. It shouldn't matter that I'm not a female he told me. A male should be in charge anyway. Females are much too emotional and flighty, he said and I agree. So he thought that if I were to impregnate you that my son would take your power and be in charge. We did a great deal of research on it and there is nothing in the books that say that it can't be a male. Killing you would be easy enough, you're a weakling and so many women die in childbirth. Then you met him."

Kyle shook his head at Maddy when she started to stand. He wanted her to appear weak in the event that he needed her. Kyle had learned one thing tonight and it was that they could accomplish more as a couple than they could as a single.

"Robert failed me in that," the man continued. "Bad, bad Robert. He was to keep you safe for me and in your place, but he failed. It took us so long to find you. That fucking bitch Heather Spring did a good job hiding you away, but going into law, that was perfect. The law! Ha! What a laugh we had over that. You see our dear dad was a lawyer, and you just followed along in his footsteps."

"She didn't want me to go into law. Grammie said that I needed to have a safer, less stressful profession. You're the reason, the reason she's dead too aren't you?" Maddy had sat up now and was leaning against the tree behind her. Kyle could see that she was stronger looking, her wounds all but gone.

"Well of course not. Robert killed her and that other woman too. But that was your fault. That woman died because you kept changing cars all the time. If you'd of just stayed in the one car, then I'd of had you sooner and that innocent woman wouldn't have been killed. So, it's entirely your fault she died. But back to me—it is all about what I'm going to do, is it not. Robert was to make sure you were not seeing anyone. He had to be punished for that. And that's your fault too. He's dead too because of you."

"You're mad. Stark raving mad," Kyle said hoping to distract him for a few seconds, diverting his attention away from Maddy. "You're a sandwich short of a picnic lunch, no air in the tires raving mad. I don't know why that surprises me, but you are." When he turned to him, Kyle leaped.

Using his extraordinary speed, he was at the man's throat in seconds. Jerking his body around so that he faced away, Kyle pulled his head up, exposed his neck and tore out his throat with the claws extending from his fingers. It was over in seconds. Dropping his body to the ground, Kyle looked up to the sky and roared in triumph.

"You'll need to take his head, Kyle." Breathing hard he turned to her voice and looked into the face of the woman he would love forever. "Take his head. If you don't, he may come back. He had enough—"

He kissed her. He'd meant only to taste her, to brush a kiss across her mouth, but one touch and he needed more. Opening his mouth over hers, he deepened the kiss and felt her respond as well, opening to him. The world faded to nothing.

An annoying yank at his arm had him pulling away much sooner than he wanted. He turned to look at Morrigan and the Fates, and growled at them.

"Later big boy. Right now we have some unfinished business to take care of. First and foremost, Madison is correct, you must remove his head. And I have to give Madison her gifts, and to you yours." Morrigan was smiling at them both. The Fates looked disappointed.

"I don't know why you couldn't let them finish," White Fate said with a pout. "It was just getting interesting. How often do we get to see a couple enjoy themselves? Never is how often. Spoil-

207

sport!" Having groused some more, the Fates moved forward as one and circled the couple.

"Melody, Queen of yada yada, come now, the night ain't getting any shorter." White Fate winked at Maddy. "See that's how it should be done, just short and simple, wham bam, thank you ma'am."

Maddy burst out laughing as did Kyle. Maddy's laughter was the sweetest sound he'd ever heard.

"You know I was in the middle of something," Mel told them as she suddenly appeared in the clearing. "A little notice next time wouldn't be remiss. Hello Maddy, Kyle. I'm so glad you were able to survive these four. Most people go batty only after ten minutes. You've been with them for nearly two hours. You should get a medal."

"Could we get started? Madison Shelby Dixon, it's time to take your place. Are you ready?" Morrigan stood before her as she asked.

"No. I don't want it."

Chapter Twenty-Six

"So now what happens?" Aaron asked Maddy again.

Kyle was lying beside her in the big bed in the MacManus mansion. Mac and Lizzy were on her other side. The entire household and friends were sitting around the room enjoying the last of the pie that Duncan had brought in only twenty minutes before.

"I have a century to be with Kyle, have children, and then we move to the other world where I become the Goddess of Fairies."

"Is that were you got this, Aunt Maddy?" Lizzy had been eyeing the armband for some time, fingering the design.

"Yes, it's a brassard. It's to protect me and to let anyone who sees it know that I am important. Would you like to see the rest of the stuff I got? It's really cool." Maddy reached under her pillow and pulled out the items that Morrigan had bestowed upon her when she'd declared her the next in line. Mel had also given her things, as had the Fates. "This is my crown, see the design? It's the Morrigan cross, I love it. It matches the tattoo that I have, and Kyle has now too."

That had been a discovery, seeing the tattoo on his chest just over his heart. She reached back now and rubbed the area, sending him warmth and love with her touch.

"This is the ceremony dagger. The Fates used it to seal the bond between Maddy and I, we cut our palms and pressed them together." Kyle held up is palm and showed the children. Maddy held hers up as well.

The dagger, like the crown was bejeweled with rubies, emeralds and diamonds. The blade was made of the purest silver, and that was why the wound on their hands had left a scar. The design on the hilt was fashioned to represent the cross.

The most prized items were the rings. Each of them wore one on their right hand. The band was made of gold, pure and gleaming. The black diamond on the top was flat with the crest of the house, the cross etched into it.

The rings held power, power beyond this world and the next. It gave Kyle the ability to be in the sun, to be able to protect Maddy at all costs. It gave Maddy the power to heal, even bring the person back from death if necessary. She'd been cautioned not to use it unless there was no other choice and she would know when that was. The rings could not be removed from their fingers ever. If someone took the finger in an attempt to take the ring, they would die a horrific death. Good to know, Maddy thought with a smile.

After another hour and Maddy yawning about four more times, the room took their leave. As they were being showed out by Kyle, Bradley stopped him and they had a quiet conversation by the door.

"What was that all about?" Maddy moved back to the bed, having come from the bathroom when he'd shut and locked the door.

"Bradley wanted to tell me something. You don't need those on" he told her when she had pulled on a tee shirt and panties to wear to bed. "I'm just going to take them off you again." The loose fitting cotton clothes suddenly felt too tight.

"I'm really tired. It's been a long couple of days." She had no intentions of not making love with him tonight, but the game was on. She moved closer to him, inches from him touching him with her body.

"Hummm, it has at that. Maybe I should go sleep elsewhere and give you some peace." Kyle ran his fingers down her arms and back up again. He tilted his head slightly as he looked at her.

"I...I don't want to make you give up your bed. Maybe I should leave you to your peace." She stepped closer now, her erect nipples brushing against his shirt. Her breath caught at the sensation.

"Madison, you try and leave this room before I'm fully sated, and I'll hunt you down and take you wherever I find you. That's a promise." She could feel his breath on her mouth, the heat of it making her dart out her tongue and moisten them.

"Kyle, what did Bradley want?" It hurt to breathe, so she began panting. It didn't help, now she could taste him as well as smell him. She moved closer still, her mouth so close to his, she could feel the heat from it.

"He told me you were ovulating, that if we wanted to, that we could conceive tonight." His lips brushed hers, just barely touching hers.

"Do you? Do you want me to carry your..." He pulled her to him, crushing her body against his leaving no doubt as to his desires.

"Madison, I want to make love to you. I want to bury my seed deep into your belly, and create a child with you. Is that what you want too?"

For an answer she stepped back from him and removed her tee shirt. Taking his hands in hers, she cupped them over her breast and moaned deeply in her chest. He leaned over her and took one hard peak into his mouth and gently nibbled. When she cupped the back of his head and pulled him closer, arching her back so that he could take more into his mouth, he opened his mouth wider and pulled more of it into his mouth.

"Please, Kyle. More, I need more." Her body hummed with need. Need for him to be inside of her and her need to take him as well.

He pushed her back toward the bed and when her calves touched the mattress she sat back on the bed. Then she lay back as he dropped to his knees before her. She felt her pussy wet and soak her panties.

"Open your legs for me, I want to taste you. I need to taste you, Love." Opening her legs she felt him move deeper between them.

He watched her watch him as he leaned down to her heat, and she thought she'd never seen anything so sexy in her entire life. When he bit into the silk that covered her mound, she felt her heart rate pick up, her blood thicken in her veins.

The panties tore away without much effort and she lay before him completely exposed. Maddy moved her hips, undulated them in a way that opened her tender lips to have her clit reveled to him. She watched him flick his tongue and taste her. Moaning deep again, she watched as he lifted her thigh and ran kisses along the inner muscle, nipping gently with his teeth. He touched one finger to her core, and then slid it inside of her, deep, curving it inside to touch her sweet spot. She creamed on his hand.

"I want to drink from you here, the taste of you feeding me and coming in my mouth is delicious." She noticed his voice was hard, gravely and low. As his mouth lowered to her, she tilted her hips to meet him, to give him what he wanted.

His tongue tunneled into her and darted in and out quickly. Her body responded by riding him, moving up and down in time with his fingers, three of them now, inside of her with is mouth suckling her clit. She reached up and cupped her breast and tugged at her nipples, pulling hard and twisting them, imaging his mouth doing this to them.

"Kyle, please…please, I need you…I need to come." She began pushing harder against his mouth, her cream and juices soaking the cover beneath them. When she felt him pull away, his fingers pumped harder faster, she knew what he was going to do. "Now, Kyle, now!"

His fangs sank into her mound, deep, and drawing his first sip of her into his mouth, her blood hot she came. Reaching down she grabbed his hair and held him close, closer as she continued to flood him with her essences and blood. He sealed the wound with a flick of his tongue, her body still writhing with pleasure. Crawling up her, fisting his cock hard in his hand, he suckled her breast into his mouth and bit her again, his teeth sinking into her nipple as he slammed his cock into her wet heat. Sucking hard he pumped into her, driving his cock deep, the painful pleasure sending her over the edge again, then again, screaming his name.

Without sealing the bite on her breast, he moved up to capture her mouth; Maddy could taste herself on his lips, on his tongue. She wanted to return the pleasure, to bite him, to drink from him. She felt the first pull of her gums, the stretching of her teeth and knew that she could. Nuzzling his neck, as he was hers she licked at the franticly beating pulse, opening her mouth wider, she sank her new fangs deep, deep into him and drank.

She felt him buck against her clit as her teeth slid in, felt his body jerk in response to her sucking her first taste of him. His cum jettisoned into her, deep and hot. When she felt him bite her throat, her world exploded, her climax gripped her so tightly and so completely that her heart stuttered to a stop and she screamed against his neck. Licking the pulse and the bite closed she wrapped her body around him and held on as the last of his tremors moved through him, his cock pulsing into her long after he had finished.

Chapter Twenty-Seven

"I have an appointment with Mr. Sherman Schaller, please." Maddy had gotten up around noon today three weeks after the incident with her brother. Only to have Duncan tell her that she had had three urgent calls from Schaller and Schaller for her to call them back. She had been asked to come by the office as her earliest convenience. She'd made arrangements to be there at three thirty.

"Please have a seat Ms. Harm. Mr. Schaller will be right out." Bimbo number sixteen was gone and in her place was an older efficient looking woman with no nonsense clothing and hair style.

"It's Dixon, not Harm. I'm married." *I suppose I should get used to saying that* she thought to herself, with a dopy grin on her face.

"Mrs. Dixon, congratulations and thank you for coming in." She hated that he had been the first to call her that, but got a thrill out of it all the same.

"Mr. Schaller. What can I do for you, if this about the breach of contract, then we—"

"Oh no, nothing like that, no not at all. I wanted to know if you'd consider coming back to work for us. I have heard that you are doing great things with B.A.C.K. Incorporated and wanted to bring you in as a full partner. This time with much better benefits and pay of course."

One of the perks that she had gotten was the new ability to read minds. And while she wasn't comfortable using it, she'd practiced some at home this morning with Sara and Duncan before coming to this appointment. She applied it now. *Oh my*, she thought.

He wanted her to become a full partner all right, but the vamp/were project would be her only client, *'no since in giving her anything else'*, he'd thought, *'being a woman she'll just fuck it up royally'*. She also learned that he had the last property in the area, paying less than one percent over the loan amount to the desperate owners. She found out he was planning to hold it as ransom until she signed over the client to Schaller and Schaller when she became an employee again.

Maddy stood up, and when he did as well she stepped forward and leaned on the desk. She'd had enough being bullied around and she was taking a stand right now.

"I want that property Shermie and I want it at what you paid for it. If you don't then I'll call your wife. I'm sure that she'd be happy to know all of the names of the bimbos that have been your mistress's over the past five years. And I want my back wages, plus interest."

It took him no more than a drawn breath to go back to the same man who had kept her under his thumb all those years. "Just who do you think you're talking to you stupid bitch? I'm not some pussy hungry sap just wait—"

"Talk like that will not endear you to me, Shermie." She had pinned him against the wall, she wasn't sure how she'd done it, but there he was. And she hadn't moved an inch. "I'm finished asking you for anything. I'm going to let you down, I hope, and you're going to call that nice woman in here and tell her just what I tell you to, understand?"

In for a pound she thought and pinched her fingers together, thinking about his scrawny little neck between them. It worked. She began to play with him, turning him upside down until all the change fell out of his pockets, mussing his hair until it stood on end. She was really having fun, too much she realized a good ten minutes later.

"All right, all right," he sobbed at her, tears falling down his face. "Please don't hurt me anymore. I'll do it, please don't hurt me anymore."

When she walked out of his office at twenty minutes after five she had the deed to the property she wanted, a check for her back wages with interest and a job reference. She didn't know if she'd need the latter. But not knowing what their finances were now that they were a couple, if she'd need to take on another job or not, but it didn't hurt to cover your bases.

She drove back to the mansion with a very light heart. Grabbing her shopping bags, she went into the house and was met by a very angry looking group of men. Not just angry but they looked positively livid. She smiled at them.

"What?" She looked at all of them, Aaron, Colin, Bradley, Kyle and Duncan. "If this is about the ticket, I assure you I wasn't speeding. Okay I was speeding, but not as fast as he said I was. Maybe. All right I was going faster than he said. But I was having a good day. The sunroof was open, and the music was too loud, I'll admit to that much. And why do you have to only go seventy five on the highway anyway? I wasn't driving stupid. Okay yes I was. One hundred and ten miles per hour is stupid, but it was—"

"One hundred and ten...You were going one hundred and ten miles per hour. Are you nuts? Aren't you the least bit...What if something had happened? You have to be certifiable that's what you are. Do you believe this?" Aaron had turned to Sara to ask her and she looked back at Maddy and winked. Maddy grinned back.

"Don't you dare encourage her" Bradley snarled at his friend. "When Officer Jones called David and told him, then he told me I nearly came after you myself. What were you thinking?" Bradley ran his hand through his hair, again from the looks of it.

"Would it help you to remember that I am immortal? And it was fun. I don't have to answer to you, to any of you. You'll do well to remember that too! Stupid men, and here I was all happy with the news I had." She tossed down her bags but not before rummaging through them and keeping one of the bags in her hand. "But oh no, there you all go, all macho and stuff, meeting me at the door like I'm some sort of...of...I don't know. But you ruined it for me. Here, I bought the last property. You all now own all the buildings in the Merchant area." She shoved the deed into Aaron's chest. Moving to Bradley she shoved the liquor licenses in his chest. "Here are two liquor licenses for the addresses we discussed. You said I could name one of the bars so it's called 'Blood Moon'. I wanted to call it 'Baying at the Blood Moon', but it was taken." She dug into the bag and pulled out a large loaf of French bread and handed it gently to Duncan. "I had to go to a different baker for this, but you said it was one of your favorites." She stood before Kyle and glared hard at him. "This must have happened before, earlier I mean. I hope you're happy with yourself." She rammed the small item into his belly and working not to drop it she stormed from the room.

~~~

Kyle looked down at what she had given him and just stared at it.

"Do you know what you have in your hand there buddy?" Aaron had come over to look at it with him.

"Not a clue. Am I supposed to?" He looked up at him and noticed the other men grinning at him.

"Hummm, I'd say she thought you should. It seems Maddy's pregnant. See that little plus sign, that means she's—" Aaron stopped talking. Kyle didn't need to hear the rest.

"Go away, I'm not finished being mad at you yet." She was in the bathroom on the floor crying.

"Madison, are you...are we...shit Madison a baby." He went in picked her up and sat her onto his lap as he sat on the toilet.

"You made me mad. I wanted to tell you tonight. I wanted it to be a surprise."

"It is, and I couldn't be happier. I love you Madison Shelby Dixon. And I've never been happier than I am right now."

"I have this too." She handed him the glowing job reference from Sherman and sat still as he read it.

"Do you not want to work for us anymore?" He stood up as he asked and carried her out to the bedroom. He laid her gently on the bed and then laid down beside her.

"I wasn't...I...we live here, and I didn't know...I know you can hold down a day job and I'm not a bad lawyer, just inexperienced. So I thought I'd work until we could find us a house, or something."

"Honey, do you think we're poor? Because we aren't. We are very, very, very wealthy. I've had fourteen hundred years to invest and collect, and save my money, just for you. I don't think we'll run out of money in several lifetimes, or more for that matter. I stay here because Aaron is my friend, but if you'd rather we stayed elsewhere, then we can certainly afford to move anywhere you want, be anywhere you want, love." He pulled her closer. He loved the feeling of her body next to his.

"No, here is fine. But I want a place before junior is born." She yawned then, big and deep.

They snuggled for a little while, his hand on her flat belly. She was nearly full asleep when the knock came at the door.

"Tell them to go away, I'm sleepy." She buried deeper into his neck, signing heavily when the knock became a pound. Kyle walked over and yanked the door open to snarl only to have everyone barge right in.

"So you thought to just give us this information and get away with going too fast?" Aaron didn't look mad to Kyle, but sometimes, like now it was hard to tell.

"Frankly, I don't care what you think about my speeding, or my driving for that matter," Maddy answered him with another yawn. "You may be old enough to be my fathers, fathers, fathers, fathers, fathers, or however many you might be, but you aren't, so back the fuck off."

"Ouch! Damn girl you go right for the jugulars don't you?" Bradley had slid into the room too. Kyle was beginning to think Maddy was right, they needed their own place.

"You do realize that the father of your baby is as old as I am, don't you?" Aaron pointed out.

"Yeah, I know. Good to know *he's* not shooting blanks, huh? Good thing for Mrs. MacManus you had one left in the old pistol."

"Why you little—" Aaron started for her.

"Keep back, you bloodsucking corpse! I mean it. I'm not in the mood to fuck with you today." Maddy had backed herself in a corner, both literally and figuratively and Kyle thought he'd like to see who came out the winner. Aaron kept going toward her.

When he stood before her, she put up her tiny fists as if to fight him. He looked down at them. Moving them out of his way, he pulled her to him and hugged her tight.

"Ah Maddy, I knew you'd be a worthy adversary the moment I saw you. I'm so happy for you and Kyle. And I'm not a corpse." He pulled back, but still held her in his embraces. "Thank you for what you've done for us, we are going to accomplish so much with your help. And just for the record, I love the name 'Blood Moon'."

"You're not mad? I don't understand you Mr. MacManus. I really don't. But you're starting to grow on me."

"Good, then will you please start calling me Aaron? I am old, but to have you call me that makes me positively want to break something."

"Yeah, I know. A girls gotta have fun," she told him with a cheeky grin.

Kyle leaned back against the door and sighed. "Do you think you assholes could get the fuck out of here? I'd like to make love with my mate and we don't need an audience."

The men all left and Kyle made his way back to the bed and Maddy. He started taking off his shirt and dropped it to the floor before he reached her. "Now, where were we?"

About the Author

I woke up one morning and decided to give play time to the people in my head who were keeping me awake. Little did I know that they would be so relentless and want their time right now! I wrote for the pure joy of it and to entertain my family and friends. But mostly it was to get more than an hour of sleep without a story playing out. Of course, the more I write, the more they want. So…well, as a result of sleepless days (I work through the night as a gun toting grandma — nope not a vigilantly but an armed security guard) I have lots of stories written.

Hello! My name is Kathi Barton and I'm an author. I have been married to my very best friend Sonny for at times seems several lifetimes — in a good way, honey. And together we have three wonderful children and then the ones we brought into the world — Paul and Dale Barton, Jason and Wendy Barton and Danielle and Ben Conklin. They have given us seven of the greatest treasures on Earth. They don't live at home seven days a week! No, seriously, seven grandchildren — Gavin, Spring, Ben, Trinity, Sarah, Kelly and Kian.

www.ingramcontent.com/pod-product-compliance
Lightning Source LLC
Chambersburg PA
CBHW020612180626
46810CB00007B/2735